COVERT THREAT

A GRAY GHOST NOVEL

AMY McKINLEY

Covert Threat

Copyright © 2019 Amy McKinley

(p) **ISBN-13**: 978-1-7339425-5-3

(e) **ISBN-13**: 978-1-7339425-4-6

Publisher: Arrowscope Press, LLC; www.arrowscopepress.com

Editing—

Taylor Anhalt, Editor

Kate B., Line Editor, Red Adept Editing

Laura B., Proofreader, Red Adept Editing

Cover Design—T.E. Black Designs; www.teblackdesigns.com

Interior Formatting & Design—T.E. Black Designs; www.teblackdesigns.com

DEAR READER,

I wanted to take a moment to welcome back the seasoned readers of this series; I'm thrilled you're back for more. If this is your first book in the Gray Ghost series, welcome to the Gray Ghost team! *Covert Threat* can be read as a standalone. Some prefer to start from the beginning, and so as not to risk any spoilers, I would recommend that as well. Either way, I hope you like the team as much as I do. And once you've finished, I'd love to hear from you.

Enjoy!
Amy

ONE

T HE STORM RAGED. DAYS LIKE those toyed with my sanity, as I was ripe with fear from a past that hovered just out of reach. Thunder boomed across the sky in an explosion that sounded like a giant whip, shaking the walls of my California beach bungalow. I sank onto a kitchen chair and wrapped my cardigan tightly around my body. A shiver coursed through me, and the small hairs along my arms rose from the electrically charged air. I curled my hands around my coffee cup, willing the warmth to seep into my chilled body.

Rattled by the intensity of the rolling waves half an acre from my bay window, I sat unblinking. The only thing that gave me even a minuscule amount of comfort were my small sips of cinnamon-and-cream-laced coffee.

Another loud boom caused my hand to jerk, and I spilled some of the hot liquid onto the kitchen table. The sky opened up in a barrage of pounding rain, hitting the roof like an onslaught of bullets. *Screw this.* Slipping my cell from my pocket, I shot off a text to my boss: *Forget the boat race.* He'd promised the weather would settle, but I knew it wouldn't.

Why did I agree to go in the first place? Oh right, bribery. We'd been promised additional funding simply for being on the yacht and in the race. Truth was, Carl was loaded, and if I'd asked, he would've given the extra funds to my team. I felt ridiculous for my commitment to participate in a team-building exercise—I was afraid of being out in deep water during any sort of stormy weather. The race wasn't about bonding, not really. Male egos were the driving force.

The waves rose and crashed against the shore, and my body trembled. Excess saliva filled my mouth, and I fought the urge to throw up. I'd worked hard with my therapist over the years, fighting tooth and nail to overcome my fears. Living near the water brought peace, and the possibility of lost years returned to fill empty memories, but violent weather over an unpredictable sea was still a no-go. My symptoms of post-traumatic stress disorder hit me hard when the ocean churned violently, bringing back the feelings of helplessness and loss from a tragic boating accident during an unexpected storm when I was young.

Another bolt streaked across the sky, and I almost fell out of my chair. My heart beat overtime. *Is that a person?* I narrowed my eyes, scrutinizing the edge of my property, where I thought I'd seen the outline of a man. Again, the sky lit up, revealing nothing unusual. I was getting too worked up over nothing.

I took another sip of coffee. *I'm safe.*

Dark clouds rolled in an ominous sky that should've been lit by then with the rising sun. A bolt of lightning violently stabbed them. Thunder answered close behind. Again, the walls shook. *God, I hate this.* Needing a distraction, I tugged on the overflowing binder I'd left out the night before. A small smile spread on my face when I touched the book, along with a surge of longing. Mom's recipes were inside.

The night before, I'd made her sauce, the perfect food to comfort me through what I thought I would have to endure today, but the race so wasn't happening. My boss had to have been certifiable. Then again, so was I to even consider stepping foot on his million-dollar sailboat. Competition did strange things to men. There were moments when I thought Carl existed merely to come up with crazy plots against Zen Pharmaceuticals. "Healthy competition," he called it, but it was far from healthy. Our team had an agreement with our rivals—we stayed out of each other's hair while our employers engaged in pissing contests.

We had pulled ahead of Zen with the large government contract we'd secured months before. Carl liked to rub that into Gary's face. We'd learned they were old college nemeses, and they were both trust-fund millionaires.

I led a team of epidemiologists and biochemists for an elite, privately owned research facility. Our research had been groundbreaking all year and had gained the attention of the US government. Carl jumped on the contract, and we forged ahead with the primary goal of keeping our military safe when on high-risk missions. When the contract expired, we were free to take the CRISPR tool kit I developed—a specific delivery method that genetically altered the CCR5 gene to become CCR5-delta 32—to the public. In doing so, we could safeguard against viral disease that accessed the immune system through the CCR5 gene.

Our lab's collective work ethic and environment were stellar. I couldn't imagine what else we needed to make us a better, more well-oiled machine.

My phone pinged, and I pulled it from my pocket, hoping the race was canceled. The excursion was an all-around bad idea. We should have been in the lab. I snorted as I skimmed over my boss's text: *It'll pass. But we'll reschedule for tomorrow to be sure.* I couldn't believe he'd even considered taking his favorite genetic epidemiologists on a sailboat race when the waves were so dangerously high. I cursed him for being an idiot and wondered whether I should agree to go.

I gave up on trying to talk sense into him and went to rinse my coffee cup before setting it in the dishwasher, hitting my side on an open drawer. I absently rubbed my hip, which I knew would bruise. I didn't remember opening that drawer, where I threw stuff I didn't know what to do with, in the first place—weird. I shoved it closed. I must have opened it by mistake last night. *I'm so spacey. Of course I did.*

From the table, I hefted the cookbook into my arms and hugged it to my chest, intent on putting it where it belonged. An empty space held the place where the book went on the shelf in my cozy living room. My hand skimmed over the worn binder that Mom and I had made years before she passed away from cancer. Even though Mom was only half Italian, she had many recipes that had been handed down from both her family and Dad's. My olive skin, something I was grateful to my parents for, was a result of generations of Italian blood.

I lifted the book carefully in my arms just as an envelope fell from its pages. My heart pounded as I fought the sheen of tears that misted over my eyes from the sight of Mom's handwriting. I set the overflowing cookbook on the table and opened it to the page that'd held the letter. Sparing a second before I put it away again, I traced my fingers over mom's flowing script, which read *Juliana*. She was the only one who'd ever called me by my full name. My nickname, Jules, had stuck hard when we'd moved from Italy to California.

With the ink beneath my fingertips, her words played through my mind: "Think of this as a sort of Pandora's box, or a Pandora's letter, if you will. Only open it—and I mean only—if strange and unexplainable things are happening. And especially if you feel you are in danger."

I had heeded Mom's warning despite my deep desire to read what she'd penned. She'd confessed that it contained a secret from our past, one my mind conveniently withheld from me. I rubbed my chest, attempting to chase the ache away. A year had gone by since she'd died, and I missed her terribly. We'd been close, and her absence left a yawning emptiness inside me, which I filled with work—it was the only thing I could do. Nothing out of the ordinary had happened, so I continued to adhere to her cryptic words.

With a deep sigh, I pushed from the table and finished getting ready. In no time at all, I found myself at the lab. Josh, the day security guard, raised his brows at me and mumbled under his breath as I breezed past him, which was odd. I glanced down at the outfit I had on. Yep, I was wearing pants —all good. I'd walked through the entrance and security check just like any other day. *Why the look of surprise?*

I doubted I would figure it out and supposed it didn't really matter. Instead, I turned my thoughts to the healing salve I was working on as I rode the elevator to my floor. In front of the secure door, I waved my badge across the access panel to enter the section occupied by the other biochemists, geneticists, and assistants on my team. The door opened with a click and a whoosh.

A few others worked at their desks and absently returned my greeting as I passed them. The starkness of the floor glared at me. Bright-white walls, desks, and glass partitions lacked warmth and personality but suited a research facility. As I rounded my desk, I came to an abrupt stop. *What the heck?* My gaze glued to an active screen saver on my monitor—the same one I knew I'd shut down before I left work the day before. It wasn't the one I had set. Instead, words scrolled on repeat across the screen: "Remember me." That wasn't normal.

"Morning." Fran walked in, running a hand over her sleek bobbed hair.

"Did you change my screen saver?"

Her brows furrowed as she slipped her purse from her shoulder. "No. Why?"

A jolt sliced through me, and instead of answering, I headed straight for my boss's office. Not waiting for a response to my knock, I turned the knob and pushed the door open. Anxiety had morphed to irritation as I figured out who'd probably messed with my computer.

Carl lifted his gaze from the papers laid out across his desk. His bushy reddish-blond eyebrows furrowed at my abrupt entry. "How can I help you, Jules?"

I curled my fingers into my palms. My nails pressed into the flesh, no doubt leaving half moons. "This team-building exercise is a mistake. It's not between you and Gary anymore. I think members of his team are retaliating against ours. Or me, to be specific." *Did he just roll his eyes?* Anger sizzled in my gut.

He glanced at my balled-up fists.

I crossed my arms and tapped my foot in response.

"And how is that?" He leaned back in his chair, his voice dripping with feigned patience.

I dropped my arms, barely stopping the huff of frustration I wanted to expel. It was going too far. He had to have been aware of what the others in the office thought about his weird rivalry with Gary—none of us liked being put in the middle of it. "When I came in a few minutes ago, my computer was on. There's a new screen saver now that reads 'Remember Me.' The words are on repeat and fill the entire screen."

His lips pulled down at the corners. "Did Fran change it? Did you leave your monitor on overnight?"

I was known to be a tad spacey. "No. I asked her, and I didn't leave it on. I'm aware of the security procedures, and it's not possible that someone could have changed it." I flailed my arms in frustration. *This is stupid.* It had to have been the other company. They could've gotten access if they were collaborating with another scientist on our floor. "My screen saver was a mix of rolling lavalike rainbow colors, not some weird message."

"I know you're conscious of security, Jules. I didn't mean to imply you'd be careless." He pushed his chair back and rose before he came around the desk. "We'll figure out what happened. Let's go see."

I resisted the urge to roll my eyes, fighting my annoyance over his careless question. I was aware of how much he respected me, and of course he needed physical proof rather than simply taking my word. My boss had a scientific as well as a business-oriented mind, and I couldn't take his need to see it himself personally.

Just under six feet tall, I had to scramble to keep up with

the much taller Carl's longer strides. We weren't far from my desk. Carl's office was only down the hall. When we made it to my station, my assistant, Fran, stood nearby, her mouth hanging open as she took in my monitor then Carl and I approaching. She must have gotten in while I was in Carl's office. Confusion flashed across her face as she briefly glanced at us. Both Carl and Fran stared at the words that scrolled across my screen in bright-green text that seemed to be mocking us.

"Do you know anything about this?" He waved his hand at the computer.

Fran looked stunned. "No. I just got here."

We stood there, clueless until Carl grunted. "Let's go back to my office, Jules." I followed him back down the hallway and into his space.

"Even you've got to admit this is strange. I mean, how did they even get in here?" I knocked my hand against his desk for emphasis. "And on top of that, do you want any of Gary's people here, where we're testing the military delta-32 project?"

"I doubt they were physically here. If at all."

You've got to be kidding me—"doubt"? We'd had incidents in the past, all in the name of good fun. Sandy, one of my colleagues whom I struggled to tolerate, was one of the pranksters. When he closed the door behind us, I pushed for the outcome I wanted most of all. "You're canceling the team-building race, right?"

He rubbed a hand over his forehead. "No." To stop the protest that was already forming on my lips, he held up his hand. "I don't think anyone from Gary's office did this. There are no collaborative projects at the moment… Although I can't understand how someone from the outside breeched our firewalls."

"Wait." My heart kicked up a gear, pounding loudly in my ears. "You think someone from outside Gary's office did this?"

"It's possible, Jules. I've heard there've been some… issues from the first test group of soldiers. Word got out about that we're administering the delta-32 tool kit to a select group and not all the units."

"What do you mean? Issues tied to the gene editing? What kind of issues?" I'd tested it countless times, and each time, it'd performed the way I'd hoped it would.

The tool kit altered a specific gene: CCR5, a coreceptor on the outside of the cell. If the procedure was performed to result in the delta-32 mutation, that person would be resistant, or immune, to many infectious diseases, such as lethal hemorrhagic fevers and even HIV. Since it was expensive to produce, we'd only been given the go-ahead to administer it to military units, per a private contract, for those soldiers who would be going into high-risk zones where enemies were known to use specific kinds of biochemical warfare. For example, we'd learned that a strain of hemorrhagic fever was being used against US soldiers, and our tool kit was one of their best defenses against it.

What I wanted to do next was work on a way to bring the costs way down and open access to the drug for everyone. Carl cleared his throat, and my focus jerked back to him.

"It may be nothing, Jules. A silly office prank." He ran his hand over his forehead. "But to be sure, I'll get our tech team on this immediately. Change all your passwords, and please be careful when you're not in the building."

What does he mean by that? Does he think I'm in danger?

TWO

THE NEXT DAY DAWNED OVERCAST and foggy with not even one storm predicted to ruin Carl's expedition. It was late September, and we were having an unusually stormy fall season. With a semiclear forecast, I found myself on board his sailboat, despite my heavy protests.

Nausea rolled in my gut as the waves fought the boat's progress through the water. Wind blew my hair back, and I shivered uncontrollably. People from work scurried around on the deck, helping. Some were getting in the way of the skeleton crew, whom Carl decided to have come with us due to our inexperience with sailing. More than just inexperienced, I hated it. It scared the crap out of me and dredged up emotions I didn't excel at compartmentalizing.

One would have thought that our presence wasn't necessary with a hired crew, but both Carl and Gary had decided the race would be forfeit, as would the bonus research money, without both teams on board. It was ridiculous.

With my legs spread wide to help myself stand on the rocking deck beneath my feet, I focused on breathing and staying out of everyone's way. Carl's sailboat cut through the water at a relatively fast pace, neck and neck with Zen Pharmaceuticals's boat.

Not much longer, I told myself. I had to hold out for maybe another half hour. The turn to head back wasn't too far ahead. A buoy with a bright-orange flag and small flashing light bobbed in the distance. Each boat had one to avoid any accidents, as it was an amateur race—a stupid race.

As we closed in on the turn, the wind died down. I pulled air in slowly and steadily, as my therapist had taught me to do during flashbacks or difficult situations. It was a major step for me to be on a boat in the overly choppy, deep water. The yacht itself was a trigger only if the weather was severe, but not nearly as traumatic as the threat the churning water presented.

Shouts rang out between the deckhands and a sparse few from my team with some experience. In a couple more seconds, we would swing around the marker, a hair's breadth behind the other boat.

A thick fog rolled in. Eerie tufts of white floated across our path, increasing in density by the second. Visibility decreased to what looked like less than a thousand meters. It seemed to get quieter as a sense of wariness permeated the air. I wanted to go home or to my lab—anywhere but on that boat.

I wrapped my arms around my stomach. John, one of the scientists on my team, stepped up to my side and gave me a tight smile. "You okay? You look a little green."

"Yeah. Not a fan of boating." I'd done my best to stay out of everyone's way. "This fog is frightening. What if we hit the other boat?" It was one of my worst nightmares and not an unfounded one—it had happened before when I was on a similar vessel.

"Don't worry. Carl is at the helm and watching the radar. We're basically on top of the turning point."

Someone called John away, and he left with a sympathetic smile. Virtually alone in an unobtrusive corner of the stern, I huddled deeper into my windbreaker. I was worried as the sailboat was heeling, a term referencing leaning that I'd learned and hoped not to experience. Wind filled the sails, and we went faster as the craft angled over the water. The waves rocked the vessel harder. Someone shouted to watch the lines. The boat lurched, tilting at an alarming level as we took the turn too fast and too tight.

My heart slammed against my rib cage. The sudden shift threw me off-balance. I staggered closer to the rail, scrambling to secure my footing. Sea spray drenched me from head to foot. Another wave hit the craft, and a heavy weight collided with my side. I lost the fight to stay on deck and flew off my feet. The boat was mid turn as my left hip struck the rail. The angle of the vessel, along with a rogue wave crashing over the bow, sent me over.

A scream lodged in my throat as blinding terror strangled my vocal cords. My body hit the unforgiving water. Darkness enveloped me as the ocean churned and swallowed me. The cold temporarily shocked my body. My lungs strained to hold air. The past collided with the present as I found myself in a similar situation to the one I'd been in as a kid. The events intermingled. Just as I had then, I clawed my way to the surface. *Please, God. Let me live.*

The surface seemed so far away, but each kick brought me closer. With every ounce of strength I could muster, I fought my way up and soon broke the surface. Gasping, I drew air into my starving lungs. I bobbed with the current, choking as the waves tossed me around. Kicking, I kept my head up. My arm shot up, and my head went under. *Shit.* The boat was quickly moving away. *No one saw me go over?*

I gasped for breath, intent to release a yell for help. A fist of salty water filled my mouth. I gagged and coughed. A minute later I tried again with little success. My scratchy voice drowned in the roar of the departing boats and rush of water.

Through the fog, I treaded water, fought the waves, and searched the deck. Water splashed in my eyes, and the fog made seeing the people on the boat difficult. I squinted through the barrage of sea spray in hope that someone had noticed and if they were, in fact, turning around to rescue me.

I was freezing. With my gaze trained on the retreating boat, another wave of sheer terror flooded me. The fog rolled in even more thickly, and in between the tufts of white, I swore I saw a familiar man near the back, leaning down. Not far behind him was a girl. *Dad?*

The boat continued to move farther away. I blinked, trying to focus. It couldn't be him. He and my sister died. It wasn't them. I swiped the back of my hand across my eyes, wiping tears and water from them.

I was going to die too. Self-preservation kept me fighting, and I searched for safety, for any way out of the nightmare. The buoy wasn't far. I could make it to that. I propelled into motion.

My arms and legs were fatigued, the cold seeping in and leeching all feeling from them. My teeth chattered as I made a desperate attempt at swimming toward the buoy, though my limbs felt heavy as concrete, and the waves pushed me further away.

A sob slipped past my shaky lips as I realized the futility. They weren't coming back. No one had seen me go overboard. I would die out there alone. Maybe I would finally see my family again.

My head slipped under, and I fought for the surface again. The buoy was farther away than I'd thought, and the waves were pushing me back with every stroke I attempted. My body was tiring. Again, I went under. Kicking with everything I had, I struggled to get above the water. The waves were so choppy. More tears came. *This is it.* I knew when I went under again, I wouldn't have the strength to surface.

A wave crashed over my head and pushed me down, and I rolled with its velocity. I held air as long as I could in my lungs —until I couldn't.

My thoughts scattered into that end-of-life kind of thing. My life flashed before my eyes.

I could see the boat. *People screamed and fell over the side. I saw him, my dad. The water tossed us around. So many of us were screaming and crying. The next time I surfaced, groggy, my head pounding from hitting it against something, I searched. He wasn't there. He must have fallen in when I was under. Arms clung to me, and I blinked. My mom's face swam into focus.*

Mom. I sobbed.

Part of me knew she'd died, but I couldn't separate what had happened before and what was in the present. *Is she here with me? Did she come to help me? Or is this the past?* I couldn't make sense of it anymore. Disoriented and hopeless, I let everything slip away: the accident, the deaths, the loneliness. *I should have died that day too. Fitting that I am now.*

Something slipped around me, pulling. Limp, I was a rag doll in its grip. It didn't matter. I was done. The air leaked from my nose, water filled my lungs, and darkness enveloped me.

I choked, spewing water. Coughing, I shook as strong arms held me tightly.

"I've got you. You're okay." A deep voice brushed against my ear. "Chris, give me a blanket."

Seconds later, a blanket was tucked around me. A man, not the one holding me, hovered above me. He had short dark hair and concerned green eyes. "Better?" he asked.

"Yes." I burrowed back against the one who held me, his body heat doing more than the blanket. I nodded, keeping the man named Chris in my sight as he retreated to the steering wheel of the speedboat—cruiser?—we were on. I wasn't sure what it was called.

The reality that I was on a different boat, held by a man I didn't know, should have been concerning, but who he was and why I wasn't dead or at least on the sailboat was too much for my traumatized mind to process.

His arms tightened, and he scooted us back along the floor of the boat. My body never moved from his, and I felt… safe. Exhausted, I sank further into his warmth and slipped under again.

THREE

MY TEETH CHATTERED, AND THE man's arms tightened around me as the boat sliced through the waves. From what he'd said, I'd blacked out for a while after he'd rescued me. My arms and legs were heavy from the ordeal, and I badly wanted to sleep. I turned toward my rescuer's chest, not wanting to face him yet but willing to shamelessly burrow into him for the warmth and safety his strong embrace offered.

Conflicting emotions battered me. It wasn't real. I mean, I did fall overboard, but it was different, I thought. As I'd nearly drowned, my mind had played tricks on me. Dad wasn't on the deck, my sister wasn't by him, and people weren't spilling over the side as I had. No one had died.

I sniffed. Tears continued to roll down my cheeks, dropping onto the blanket tucked tightly around me that blended into the one draped across his wet shoulders. The scent of ocean and man seeped into my senses, and I calmed, at least enough to stop crying. I was fine aside from the cold and a headache. *They were just flashbacks. Everything will be okay.*

The roar of the motor slowed, and we coasted. The waves slapped against the side of the boat. We pulled up to the docks, and Chris jumped off to secure us. I didn't want to move. The man who held me threw off a lot of heat, which I badly needed. His arms stayed firmly around me as I remained tucked against his solid chest. He made me instinctively feel safe, and I didn't even know who he was.

Chris came back into view, jumped onto the deck, and sat in a seat facing us. Elbows to knees, he leaned forward. "How are you feeling?"

"Okay." I cleared my raw-from-screaming throat. "Better."

"The boat you were on just docked." He glanced past my shoulder to the man I leaned against.

"Are you ready to get up?" My rescuer's deep voice rumbled in his chest and sent a different kind of shiver through me.

I nodded. But no, I wasn't.

In one smooth motion, he rolled to his feet from where we'd sat on the deck without releasing me. I slid down a little as he stood. My head barely reached his shoulder.

"We need to get you warm." He lifted me fully into his embrace. I would have protested, but my legs were jelly, so I couldn't.

"I got the boat," Chris called to us as the man holding me jumped from the side to the dock with me firmly cradled in his arms. I needed him to put me down before anyone on my team saw. Well, soon at least, anyway. He was far too comfortable.

"Oh no! Jules!" *Too late.* A group of women from my team crowded us, forcing me to turn my head from his warmth.

No one met my eyes. *What's going on?* I frowned at the fake concern coating their voices then followed their gazes to the man who held me. I sucked in a breath. *Holy shit.* Dread filled me. He'd tilted his head down, and his laughing eyes caught mine. *No, no, no, no.* The pilot who'd flown my boss and me to DC a few times was my rescuer, the very one who'd shamelessly flirted with our flight attendant. It'd been so uncomfortable with the whispers, the laughter, and her blush-stained cheeks.

Heat from embarrassment pushed some of the chills away as I took in his broad shoulders, strong chin, and chiseled face —he was as gorgeous as Ben Dahlhaus. It was annoyance, I told myself. I was feeling irritation, not attraction. Definitely not.

I dragged my gaze back to the ladies on my team, who were all traitors. They weren't concerned that I'd fallen over-board and suffered a flashback to before I lost my dad and sister. No, they only wanted to get close to Trev Shaw, the man who held me and apparently all their fantasies. They were idiots. Seriously—a group of brilliant women was fangirling over a guy. I'd heard them enough times, gushing about him after Sandy had gone out with him once. At least only three of my colleagues, Sandy, Linda, and Melissa, had morphed into teenagers. Even so, they were highly intelligent people who worked under me, and at the sight of a handsome man with muscles and charm leaking out his ears, they turned into adolescents. It was an embarrassment to working females everywhere.

"Jules!" Carl's deep voice boomed over my simpering colleagues as he jogged from the boat toward us. *Will my humili-ation never end?* The women continued to fawn over Trev, asking if he was okay and praising him for rescuing me. I had to fight to stop from rolling my eyes.

I pushed against his chest, but he didn't budge. His arms remained locked around me. "Let me down." I refused to look at him. I was grateful to him but in no way going to join his fan club. As he lowered me to the ground, I put some necessary distance between us. The women around us closed ranks.

Huffing, I stepped outside their ring of adoration and came face to face with Carl. His hands clasped my arms, which were shivering again.

"What happened?" Concern swam in his eyes, and some of the tension in my shoulders eased.

"I'm not entirely sure. When the boat turned and that big wave hit, I lost my footing." My shoulder and hip throbbed, reminding me what else had happened. "Something slammed into me from behind, and I went over."

The color drained from his face. "What hit you?"

I shrugged. "No idea. Whatever slammed into me was pretty hard. Could have been gear that'd come loose, or maybe someone else lost their balance and bumped into me?"

He shook his head. "Well, I'm glad you're okay."

"Did you see me go over?"

"No. Fran yelled that you'd fallen over, but after we rushed to the rail to see where you were, Trev had dived off his boat and was swimming toward you. When I saw that you were safe and he was bringing you back to his boat, we headed in."

Thank God for my assistant. A shoulder bumped me, sending a fresh surge of pain through it. "Sorry, Jules." A warm hand squeezed my arm as Fran leaned close. "I'm so glad you're okay. And wow, if I'd known he was near, I might have jumped overboard too." Fran grinned before she shoved herself in between Sandy, who was vying for a better position next to Trev, and me.

Brainwashed and hormonal groupies surrounded me.

Wait—why is he here? "Carl." I narrowed my gaze at him, despite my shivering. "Why would Trev have been here too? He's not part of our team."

Carl grunted and avoided my question. "Ladies, head over to the picnic area."

No one moved.

"Now."

A few of the women grumbled as they left to go to the wooded picnic area, where the others had gathered after learning I was okay. I was freezing, and I could not afford to get sick. I would give him a few seconds at most to answer. "Carl, please tell me why he's here before I head home."

He awkwardly patted my shoulder. "Of course. Give me a minute to explain. Trev"—he motioned for my rescuer to come closer—"I asked you to meet with us here about a security risk we learned of this morning."

I couldn't deal. I wanted to go home and forget the day.

"Carl, I need to go. I'm sure this morning was some weird prank from one of the Zen scientists."

"I don't think so, Jules." He turned to Trev. "We have a possible military breach. After talking it over this morning with Rich Stevens, who coordinated our involvement with the soldiers and branches, he and I thought you would be the best person for the job. I appreciate you meeting me here today."

This isn't happening. I wrapped my arms around my waist, knowing exactly where the conversation was headed. "I don't need a babysitter." And I doubted it was one of the soldiers; Carl was being paranoid. It had to be one of the other scientists. I narrowed my eyes and turned to Trev, who was observing me with an expression I couldn't decipher. "No offense to you. I'm sure the incident was nothing. A harmless joke."

"None taken." His deep voice rolled over me, playing me like a fine-tuned instrument.

I needed to go. "Carl, I'm getting another headache, and I'm freezing and can't get sick—you especially wouldn't want that. I'm going to bail on the rest of the activities planned for today. Trevor, thank you again for pulling me out of the ocean." I turned on my heel and hurried as quickly as my legs would carry me, as far from them as I could get. The day needed to end.

TREV

JULES RUSHED AWAY WITHOUT A backward glance. She was different—she intrigued me. Once she was in her car, I faced her boss to find out what he wanted. If it meant spending some time with the one woman who seemed to be immune to me, I wanted in. She was a puzzle I wanted to figure out.

"So you talked to Rich?" Rich Stevens was our government contact for Gray Ghost Security, a private military team my brother and I were a part of, along with several guys we grew up with and a few from our time as active Navy SEALs. We were basically family.

I sized up Carl Aldridge. I'd flown him and Dr. Jules Moretti once or twice at Rich's request—Rich had described something to do with military-exclusive vaccines. Both times, she'd ignored me after a polite greeting. Jessica had been the flight attendant, and for some reason, Jules had seemed irritated when we'd joked around. I'd caught her subtle glares but had no idea what I'd done to deserve them. Jess was a friend, and I had been teasing her about her boyfriend. I wasn't sure what Jules heard or what it had been about my hushed discussion with Jess that had set her off.

I could admit that Jules was a beautiful woman, but she'd seemed cold and standoffish before. But after I rescued her and held her in my arms, the good kind of sparks flew between us. It was unexpected and confusing, something I hadn't experienced much in the past, at least not to that degree. Her silky skin was like a live wire beneath my fingers. I wanted time to figure out what the pull between us was.

"Yes, I talked with Rich." Carl broke into my thoughts, and I focused on him. "I also spoke with Gary from Zen Pharmaceuticals, and he confirmed that none of his scientists had conferred with my team the night before or the morning of the screen-saver problem. To give you some more background, Jules is spearheading a top-secret gene-editing procedure that only a handful of soldiers are receiving at this time. While I believe this problem comes from within our company, given our firewalls, I cannot rule out outside threats." He rubbed the back of his neck and pressed his lips into a thin line. "She is vital to my company, and I need someone to guard Jules."

"And since I've flown her a couple of times and live close to

Thorn Pharmaceuticals, Rich thought I'd be the best man for the job?"

"He did. And I want to stress that Jules is invaluable to my department. The company. No one can do what she can. I want her protected even if this turns out to be some strange office prank."

"What exactly happened?"

Carl shoved his hands into the pockets of his khaki pants. "It sounds odd to worry about this, but I don't like to take chances with my employees' safety, especially hers. There was a message that said 'remember me' on her computer, scrolling across her screen on repeat. It was in that old-school bright green on a black background. It was unsettling." Carl seemed worried.

"Do you have an idea of who could have done it and what it could mean?" It didn't seem overly threatening to me, but I didn't have all the details yet.

"That's the weird part. Since we are a privately owned company, our security is tight, like government-level secure. It had to be someone on the inside unless our servers were breached, which would be next to impossible, but everyone likes Jules. I've never heard a negative word about her."

"You're the boss, though, and you might not hear everything. You know how people are. Unless complaints were brought directly to you, there's no way for you to know for sure if someone has a problem with her."

Carl rocked back on his heels, pausing for a moment. "I see what you mean. We've kept this breakthrough in strict confidence between our team and a select few military personnel. Our IT department has assured me that no one accessed our servers from the outside. Even so, I had them make changes to tighten security further. I have a bad feeling about this. Jules was the one to administer a new vaccine to two groups of soldiers." He shook his head. "What if one of the personnel members she came into contact with learned about the restricted procedure and is sending her the message? There were a few people not on the list that were talking with her."

Someone laughed in the distance, and I glanced to where the rest of Carl's team had gathered in a picnic clearing before facing him again. "So you think it could be one of the soldiers she came in contact with? One who had above average hacking skills and had a crush on her and is stalking her?"

"Maybe. I'm not sure. It's just that the message seemed personal. It rattled her. Jules was white as a sheet. Then she got an intense headache."

"Do you think she knows who is behind this but isn't telling you?"

"No." Carl sighed, his face drooping, and he suddenly looked as though he'd aged five years. "Jules suffered a tragedy when she was young. Because of the trauma and a head injury, she can't recall anything from before that time."

"And you think this has something to do with the message on her screen?"

"No, I don't. I think the message has to do with someone who developed a weird obsession with her. I just felt the need to explain a little about her past and the cause for the headaches… They also happen when she's stressed."

"I understand." Chris had suffered a head injury, too, and had described such discomfort if he tried to remember before the memories were ready to resurface. "The headache was probably either from the stress of the potential threat or because her memories were close to the surface. Maybe before she was ready?"

"Yes. She was frightened, but that's not something she would admit. I think the shock gave her the headache."

I widened my stance and crossed my arms over my chest, eager to find out what it was he wanted. "What exactly are you hiring me to do?"

"If you agree, I'd like you to guard her. Drive her to and from work. Try to figure out how someone got access to her computer. With your connections, it shouldn't be hard to weed out who's targeting her, especially if it was someone she encountered prior to or after administering the injections. I need you to make sure nothing happens to her."

"So a bodyguard."

"I know you were a Navy SEAL and about the private security company you're a part of. I think you have the skills necessary to keep her safe."

It took about two whole seconds to make up my mind. I needed something to do outside of the women's self-defense classes I was teaching, which I was doing because I felt like I needed to empower women, given what my mom had gone through. Aside from that, I was free, and boredom was not my friend—it never had been. Plus, she was an enigma, and I was determined to figure her out.

"We can sit down and iron out the details after the team-building meeting scheduled for the rest of the day, if that works for you." Carl's eyebrows appeared to climb his forehead as he waited for my response.

"I'll want to bring some of my guys on to help me narrow down the list of suspects."

Carl grinned. "Whatever needs to happen. She is the jewel of this company. The work she is doing has pulled us leagues ahead of the competition, securing Thorn Pharmaceuticals as one of the top research and development companies around. I can't afford to have anything happen to her."

FOUR

S WEAT DRIPPED FROM MY FACE and rolled down my chest until it hit my sports bra. My body ached in a good way. Imagine Dragons crooned in my ears, and I dropped the mat to the floor before sitting on it. Bending forward, I grabbed my toes and stretched. The pain from the day before was gone, except for the bruise on my shoulder blade. I'd decided to put the plunge into the ocean behind me. I'd done the meditation exercises that I'd learned and practiced for years, and I felt better.

Switching positions, I pulled my heels in and leaned over my bent legs and toes, humming to "Bad Liar." An odd note filtered into the chords, and I yanked an earbud out to listen.

The doorbell rang again. Weird—I wasn't expecting anyone. I rolled to my feet, went to the door, and opened it. Tall, muscular, and handsome filled my field of vision.

"What are you doing here?" I crossed my arms over my chest, annoyed that he'd caught me sweating through my sports bra and running shorts.

He grinned and hooked his hands above his head on the top of the doorway in the position men seemed to universally take to drive women nuts or cause spontaneous drooling. It worked. My heart rate kicked up a notch. Muscles bulged in his arms, and his eyes sparkled. He knew what he was doing. I narrowed my eyes. *It's not gonna work.*

"Remember the conversation Carl had with us before you left?"

Shoot. I did, and it was silly. "Do you think this is necessary?"

"Your boss does."

He grinned, and I backed up a step and tripped over my own feet. *Dammit.* He caught my elbow to steady me. He was too big, too handsome, and just too much. Having him in my house was not okay. I didn't need distractions, and he was one.

"I'm fine." I pulled my arm away, not thrilled about the zaps of awareness that danced along my skin from where he'd held me. "Come in, I guess."

His smile widened at my obvious irritation, which only further flustered me. He closed the door behind him, and my irrational temper flared. "Make sure you hear the click when you shut the door. If not, it'll open if there is a strong gust of wind."

The hairs along my arms raised in uncomfortable aware-ness of how much space he seemed to take up in my small beach house. "We need to establish ground rules if I'm going to agree to this."

"Do we, now?" He chuckled.

I sucked in some air. I needed patience to deal with the situation, which was occurring before seven in the morning. It was seriously too much for Carl to put on me. I held out a hand and started ticking off on my fingers what I would allow. "First, you are not going to go to work with me. Second, I'm not sure what encompasses bodyguard hours, but I'm not okay with you sleeping here. Third…" *Shoot, what else do I want?* My mind went blank. I needed coffee. I was still tired. I glared at him before turning and stomping into the kitchen to start the fuel necessary to function.

"So no third."

I jumped, not having heard him enter the kitchen behind

me. When I glanced at him over my shoulder, I caught his grin as he stood in the entryway. I rolled my eyes.

"Any other demands?"

"Yes. I'll think of more." I filled my cup with coffee then pointed at the mug to see if he wanted any. He shook his head. After adding cream and cinnamon, I waved my hands, ushering him back into the other room. "What is it you've been asked to do for this job?"

"Drive you to and from work, make sure you're safe, and look into the screen-saver incident. Sounds easy enough."

"Oh, okay. So you're not going to be around all the time?"

"Not unless something changes, no."

That didn't seem too bad. I didn't like it, but I could put up with his presence for a while. The weird screen-saver prank would fade from memory, and Carl's worry would blow over. Then I'd be back to my normal routine of working and running, rinsing, and repeating. Distracted, I pointed at the kitchen. "I've got to get ready for work. Help yourself to food or coffee."

I left him standing in the living room. I closed my bedroom door and leaned against it. *What the hell am I going to do with him following me to and from work?* Scrubbing my face with the bottom of my shirt, I groaned. He was sex on a stick, and the women in my office were *not* immune. He couldn't come up to look into the screen-saver issue. We wouldn't get any work done if he was around. I grinned. He and I were going to set some more ground rules, no matter what he'd agreed to with Carl.

After a quick shower, I threw on some clothes, ready to head back to the living room to have a chat with Trev. I stepped in front of the mirror and froze. *Holy shit.* The glass was steamed up except the words "remember me before it's too late" written across it.

This isn't funny. I sucked in a breath, left the bathroom, and pressed my back against my bedroom wall. My head throbbed as a headache spontaneously struck. I left my room and made it halfway down the hall before stopping. *Did I really see that?* I had to be sure. With the way my head pounded, I couldn't be sure. Tiptoeing back to my room, I made my way to the bathroom and stood before the mirror. Nothing was there. No words. It had been my imagination. It had to be.

SEVERAL HOURS PASSED WHILE I worked in the lab, effectively banishing all thoughts of Trev and the imagined mirror incident, at least for the most part.

I had planned to tell him when I'd first left my room, but that changed when I went back into the bathroom and the writing was gone. I'd even run the sink until steam coated the surface once more, but nothing appeared. It had to have been my imagination. I was too embarrassed to confide in anyone about it. I would have to make an appointment with my therapist. She would know what was going on. It was probably just stress.

"Jules! Fran!" Carl's bellow momentarily halted work in the lab.

Questioning gazes from colleagues clashed with ours as we stepped away from the table where we were working. I answered their silent inquiries with a shrug—their guess as to what had him all riled up was as good as mine.

Fran bumped my shoulder. "Any clue what this is about?"

"None." Exiting the lab, we rounded the corner to Carl's office.

A deep frown etched lines across his forehead and bracketed his mouth.

"What's going on?" A sense of dread stirred in my gut. He looked distressed, an expression he rarely wore.

"I just got off the phone with Dr. Mikhailov. He's hoping

for aid in solving a major problem in regards to a tragedy they've suffered."

"Okay," Fran murmured as she looked back and forth from Carl to me.

"One of his lab technicians, Sasha Orlova, was working in the field where a dead body from centuries ago was discovered in the melting permafrost in the Yakutsk region." Carl scrubbed his hand over his face before his wide eyes met mine. "Sasha was exposed to the infectious pathogens by villagers who were in contact with the thawed gravesite before the scientists recovered the body. At least that's what we've determined."

A sense of dread warred with my need to unravel what'd happened. I could read his body language clearly. Whatever Orlova had encountered, which had been frozen and preserved so long ago, hadn't resulted in a positive outcome.

"She's dead." He cleared his throat as I dropped like lead into a chair in front of his desk. "Dr. Mikhailov is imploring us to contribute our expertise so that his employees stand a chance of survival. I met him at a conference a year or so ago. Jules, he heard of the research and findings you've conducted surrounding monoclonal antibodies. It might help them."

"How did she die? What were her symptoms?" I had to know to even hypothesize a course of action.

"Dr. Mikhailov thinks it could have been a strain of hemorrhagic fever. We're not sure which one. It could have been an ancient variant we haven't yet seen."

If it's one we haven't encountered before, we might not have a defense for it. My stomach clenched at the thought of what Sasha would have experienced before she died. Fast-acting hemorrhagic fevers caused severe dehydration, nausea, and diarrhea, and as the symptoms worsened, victims often experienced severe pain. It could've attacked her pancreas and liver along with damaging blood vessels and causing massive hemorrhaging. It wasn't a pretty way to go.

"What's happened to the villagers and the scientists working on this find?" Fran asked.

Carl cleared his throat before pulling himself together, all business once again. "They've been quarantined—"

"They want access to our military-grade tool kit?" No, that wasn't it. They wouldn't have known about that project. "They want the antibodies to combat foreign pathogens." Shock had slowed my processing time. My second answer made the most sense—I knew it would create the best-case scenario for their survival.

Carl nodded. "They've delivered sealed samples for us to run tests on. As quickly as this infection has seemed to spread, we need to be extremely careful."

"I understand. When can I start working on it?"

"Immediately. The biopsies were sent over by secured courier this morning. I'm assigning you and Fran to spearhead this, and a separate team at Zen will work on discovering a cure as well. We're combining forces to help them."

To help us all. Undiscovered viruses or plagues would affect more than that tiny region. It could become a world problem. "Are there any other companies involved?" I couldn't imagine that Carl's company, Thorn Pharmaceuticals, and his rival, Zen Pharmaceuticals, were the only two willing to offer their time.

"I'm unaware of who else is involved. Let's do what we can on our end." Carl rapped his knuckles on his desk. "Get to work."

Fran and I stood and filed out of Carl's office then made our way toward our workspace. She turned to me and spoke in a hushed tone. "We're going to have to work fast. You know what this could mean, right?"

I mentally prepared for the hours of intense work we would do today and kissed the run I planned along the beach tonight goodbye. A sense of urgency coated my response. "Yes, a potential outbreak."

FIVE

Exhaustion clung to my movements from the long
hours in the lab the day before as I wrung out my dark-
brown hair before wrapping it in a towel. The combination of
the melting permafrost ramifications and the small amount of
sleep I'd gotten made me shaky and anxious about what else
could happen. Flashbacks from the message on the mirror the
day before taunted me, and a slow ache built in my head. *I can
do this.* Taking a deep breath, I looked at the mirror. Condensa-
tion coated the unspoiled surface. I sighed in relief. Nothing
stared back at me.

I took a deep breath then walked out of the bathroom and
picked up my phone. I'd left a message for Trev about when I
would be ready. We'd agreed the day before that he would
shadow me everywhere except on my morning runs. I wanted
those for myself   I needed some time on my own.

I heard a muffled click, which pulled me from my room
and into the hallway. "Trev?" It sounded like a door, but I'd
locked the front entrance. He wouldn't have let himself in, I
didn't think.

Goose bumps crawled over my skin. It was creepy—I was
either hearing things, or someone was in my house. With my
phone clutched tightly in my grasp, I went from room to room.
After clearing the kitchen, I breathed a sigh of relief. My mind
was playing tricks on me again. No one else was there.

I did a quick time check and cursed when I realized I only

had five minutes before Trev would arrive. Back at my closet, I stood in front of my clothes, at a loss for what to wear. I never had that problem, and I wondered what my deal was, given that I wore a lab coat every day. There was no reason to put on a skirt, even though I liked the pretty pale-yellow-and-blue-flowered print. It certainly was not because I would see Trev. My face heated.

I settled on pants and a blouse. After blow-drying my hair, I put on a minimal amount of makeup. The doorbell rang, and I dropped the mascara brush. *Shit.* A smear of black marred the white sink. I shoved the wand back in the tube and tossed it onto the counter. *I'll clean that later.*

I yanked open the front door, and my pulse kicked up a notch, which was not okay. He leaned against my doorframe, his eyebrows furrowed, and I took a step back, wondering whether he was irritated. I couldn't focus. With a jerk of my head, I let reality slap me in the face. He was *not* for me. I recognized the attraction for what it was—he made me feel safe and protected. After all, he had saved me from drowning.

After rationalizing my reaction to him, I flashed him a brief smile as I ticked through the list of what I had to do for work. "Coffee." I waved him in. "I need some. You?"

"You always open the door without checking to see who it is?"

I rolled my eyes then turned my back on him and headed into the kitchen. "Okay, Dad." I got it—he and Carl were worried about me. But it had to be the other company trolling me. One year, they'd replaced all our lights with strobes. Carl was forgetting the stuff that sometimes went on. Initially, I had been upset about my computer being touched and thought the message was strange, but there had to be an explanation. It had to be someone playing tricks with Sandy's help.

As I poured coffee into a travel mug, he bent over and picked up one of my gym shoes. "What's this? You went jogging?" He held my damp running shoe, and a few grains of sand fell from the sole.

With a slap to his hand, I moved the smelly sneaker away as annoyance sizzled through me. "Look, I agreed to you shadowing me back and forth to work. I'm *not* answering to you about everything I do. This is not negotiable and completely unnecessary."

He crossed his arms over his chest. I rode the anger, refusing to let him distract me with his impressive biceps, which had grown even bigger in that position. "It's probably some ridiculous game Zen is playing. They've pranked a few of our team members before when there was a prize to win. Did Carl tell you about that?"

He smirked. "Yeah, I know about the research-money competition. I also know that Carl's college buddy runs the other company, and they have an unhealthy competition once a year. The other pranks weren't like this. And you know it."

"Doesn't mean a screen-saver prank is unheard of." I was worried about my overactive imagination—the mirror episode was a prime example. I wasn't willing to let him know, as it made me look crazy. Maybe I was under too much stress. If something significant happened, I would tell him, but even I wasn't ready to fully acknowledge my craziness.

"I'm ready. Let's go." I turned my back on him to grab my bag from the table. Panic held me prisoner. It wasn't there. Maybe I did hear someone enter earlier, and they'd stolen it.

Slowly, I turned to face Trev. He reacted. A hard glint shone in his eyes, his lips pressed into a firm line. He took a step forward, and his hands curled around my arms as he pulled me toward him. "What's wrong?"

Okay, that reaction was different and revealed a side of him that was downright scary, but oddly, not to me. His nearness eased the fear swimming in my gut. I told him what was missing. "My keys and my purse were right there on the table. I even saw them this morning before I went running. I *know* I didn't move them."

"Was your door unlocked when you came back?"

"No."

"Did anything else unusual happen last night or this morning?"

I should tell him at least one thing. "I thought I heard the door open when I was getting ready, but it was nothing. I searched the house." I settled on part of the truth. The mirror still seemed too personal. I wasn't sure I wanted to tell him, especially since I'd had such a hard time believing it myself, and we barely knew each other.

"Let's see if your stuff is somewhere else in the house."

I followed him until he stopped in front of the living room couch. I peeked around. *What the hell?* My bag was on the coffee table.

No. I knew I didn't leave the bag there. Sheer panic flooded my system, and I turned to face Trev. "It wasn't here before. I swear."

His face gave nothing away, aside from the intensity in his eyes, which didn't seem typical for him. He was easygoing and charismatic. "You heard the door open when you were in your bedroom?"

"Yeah, but the doors were locked, and I searched the house. No one was here. I thought it was my imagination, but now I'm not so sure." A shiver ran along my skin.

He gave my arm a gentle squeeze. "Give me a few minutes."

I jerked half a step forward, reached out, and gripped his hand with my own. "You're leaving?"

"No." He pulled his hand away and guided me to the couch. "I'm looking through your house one more time. I want you to go through your purse and make sure nothing is missing."

That made sense. I opened it up and dumped the contents

out while he went from room to room. It wouldn't take long. The house was small.

As I was putting everything back, he sat opposite me.

"Nothing's gone." My hands trembled as I put the strap on my shoulder, tightly clutching my keys in my other hand.

He shook his head. "After work, we're coming back here, and I'm going to install some outdoor cameras and motion-sensor lights." He stood. "Come on, let's get you to work."

I let him pull me to my feet, and we headed out the door. Doubt crept in. *Could I have moved my stuff?*

He flashed me his signature crooked grin as he held the car door open for me. "Everything will be okay."

I wasn't so sure.

THANK GOD FOR WORK. I was lucky that I loved what I did, which made the day fly by. The virus was definitely a hemorrhagic RNA virus, ancient in origin. Sasha's death had not been an easy one. It wasn't a virus we had encountered before, and it didn't have a cure—that's where the antibodies came into play. Our first battery of tests would unpack the virus itself. The next step was to see if the virus would be able to infect genes with the delta-32 mutation.

Before I knew it, Trev was texting me that he was parked in front of the building. I glanced at the time and realized it was time to pack up for the day.

After shutting down my workstation, I went back into the lab to straighten up. "It's getting late, Fran. Let's call it a day."

When she turned from the vials we had lined up, I felt immediately guilty. She looked exhausted. Her usual sleek bob was a mess, half moons hung beneath her deep-brown eyes, and her usually pale skin looked drawn.

"Are you okay?"

Fran offered a tired smile. "I am. Just a late night."

I tucked the last vial into the specimen container then picked it up.

Fran intercepted with a wide grin, infusing some life back into her expression. "You know better than that, Grace."

"We're still doing that?" I'd never lived it down. I'd tripped one time too many and lost hours of work, and Fran started calling me Grace for the lack of it that I possessed.

"Of course we are. I'm not pulling an all-nighter because you think you can safely put this away—across the room? There are so many things you could trip over. Like your feet." She winked. "I've done too many of those with you."

Grumbling, I washed out the beaker and placed it on the shelf with the others. "Fine." It was embarrassing as hell but true. "But you can stop calling me Grace. No need to give my unfortunate clumsiness a nickname." I leaned a hip against the counter and waited for her to lock the fridge storage where we kept the tool kit for the military. If needed, the vector—also known as a genetically engineered carrier—had a thirty-day shelf life without refrigeration.

Once everything was safely stored away, she came to my side. "You know I love you, right? I keep things real, and you love that about me." She chuckled. "You're a klutz *and* a space case, but it's not because you truly lack grace. It's because you're brilliant, and your mind is constantly coming up with amazing solutions."

My eyes went blurry, and I blinked away the excess moisture. She was sweet. I was fortunate to have her as an assistant and a friend. "Thanks."

She lifted a shoulder and let it drop. "It's true. I'm lucky to be able to work with you."

"Now you're just kissing my butt." We hung up our lab coats and headed out. "Reviews are coming up, aren't they?"

Her eyes went wide. "What? I forgot all about them."

I burst out laughing as Fran feigned surprised innocence. I

would be in charge of her review, and it was fun to make her sweat a little. "Later, Franny."

She shook her head before turning toward a little café we occasionally ate at. "Later, Brainy," she said over her shoulder.

I scanned the cars parked in front of the building until I found Trev's black Range Rover. He got out, and I sucked in a breath, thankful that Fran was already out of sight. That morning, she'd harassed me with questions about him, what it had been like to be rescued by him and to be in his arms. I'd shut it down quickly, and she hadn't brought it back up yet, though I knew it was a matter of time. It was annoying but revealed how I felt around him—off-balance. I didn't want to admit it to Fran or myself.

As he came around the SUV, I stepped closer. Damn that crooked grin—it suited him, and I understood why so many women made fools of themselves around him. Not me, though. I wasn't going to fall prey to his charm. Careful not to brush against him, I avoided the hand he offered to help me into the vehicle. Because honestly, from my previous experiences with him, tingles followed every place he touched. "I'm fine."

"Just offering a hand, *Brainy*."

I jerked my gaze back to his. "Are you making fun of me?" Fran was allowed to tease me—we had history. I didn't know him, not really.

He frowned before shutting my door. Once he was back in the driver's seat, he turned to me. "Not maliciously. But yeah, I was teasing you. Your boss couldn't stop talking about how valuable you are to the company, and then your assistant called you Brainy. Seems like a good nickname."

I shifted in my seat, wondering where a wormhole was when I needed one. "Carl is obsessing again, his eyesight firmly on the company profits. I'm not better than any of the other people working for him."

"I picked up dinner and a temporary camera for your doorbell."

I let him change the subject, relieved to be off that topic. "Temporary?"

The light turned, and he punched it, shooting us ahead of the other cars. "This one will do the job in a pinch, but my brother will come through with much better and more reliable ones. I'll install those tomorrow."

My stomach growled. I pressed my hand against it, hoping he hadn't heard.

No such luck. "Hungry?" Laughter practically dripped from his question.

"I forgot to eat lunch. What did you pick up?"

He pulled into the driveway and shut off the engine. "Chinese. Hope that's okay."

"MSG?" I'd texted him back earlier today when he'd asked if I had any food allergies or dislikes. He knew about my MSG sensitivity, but I wanted to make sure, as the repercussions from it weren't pleasant.

"I know a guy there. He swore they didn't use any."

"Better not have. If they lied, you'll be taking care of me while I'm suffering from a massive migraine."

"You got it."

I hopped out of the truck before he could come around and help me. After I unlocked the door, we walked inside.

Trev put a couple of plastic bags on the kitchen table and the rest on the counter. I set two plates and glasses of water on the table and rummaged through the bags, pulling out containers of food and wondering how much he thought I would eat.

We piled our plates high with Kung Pao chicken, fried rice, wontons, and egg rolls then dug in, comfortable with the silence. After almost half of the food was gone, mostly consumed by Trev, I couldn't stifle my curiosity anymore. "Why did you take this job? You're a glorified babysitter and chauffeur. I know you have skills better used elsewhere that make driving me to and from work laughable."

He finished chewing and set his chopsticks down. "There was this look you had the day I fished you out of the ocean. Haunted. Lost. It reminded me of an aspect of my past." He flashed a closed-lipped smile. "That's a story for another time."

My body stiffened when he mentioned the vulnerability he'd glimpsed from me that day. But he seemed to have his own demons, and though intrigued, I decided to let it drop—mostly. "What can you tell me about your past?" Since I couldn't tell him much about mine, thanks to the amnesia, I wanted to hear his.

"This will probably offend your sense of ethics." He winked. "My brother is off-the-charts smart when it comes to anything technological. When we were young, he'd hack into the school computers and alter the financial-aid records to get my family through hoops so we could get things like free lunch, waived registration fees, those types of roadblocks. It made getting an education and eating possible."

"Was he older or younger?"

"Older, but not by much. Anyway, one day, I wanted to mess with him. As I said, Chris was—is—crazy smart. Of course, he'd aced every assignment in his tech class. So I hacked into the school's system and changed the last one from an A-plus to a C."

I laughed. I couldn't help it. "You didn't."

His eyes sparkled with mirth. "Oh, I did, and he was pissed. As soon as he saw it, he beat my ass."

"Wow." They had to have been a handful for their parents. I laughed with him at the picture he'd painted. "I honestly don't know what to say."

"Do you have any siblings?"

My smile fell from my lips. "I had a sister."

"Had?"

"When I was young, my family and I were in a boating accident in Italy, where we lived. My mom and I moved to the States after. I was barely a teenager, and it was too hard for her.

The accident… There was an unexpected storm, and the water was so rough. The day of the collision, I lost my dad, my sister, and my memory of everything before."

"I'm sorry."

I shrugged. "My mom and I were thrown over together. So many had fallen overboard like us. Another boat was going too fast and couldn't turn quickly enough in the choppy water. They lost control and slammed into the side of ours. And the waves—God, they were huge that day. Anyway, I hit my head pretty bad. I mostly can't remember what happened before I fell over. Everything started from bits and flashes but then turned mostly normal once I was fully conscious in the hospital bed."

"Mostly?"

I worried my lower lip with my teeth, weighing the idea of opening up to him as he had with me about his brother, at least a little, and it hadn't painted him in a favorable light. I could try to be vulnerable to him too. "While I was in the water before you pulled me out, I had a flashback of that day in Italy."

"What did you remember?"

He hadn't moved since I'd started talking. The intensity had returned, pushing his easygoing persona to the backseat. The man before me exuded a barely leashed power—it was overwhelming, intimidating.

"I was confused," I said. The images flashed again, and I flinched. "When I looked at the boat, it wasn't the same sailboat, but the one I was on with my parents. In one blink, they were on the deck, blurry—my dad and sister. In the next, they weren't. I couldn't tell where I was, whether I was in the past or the present, or what was going on." I shrugged again, pushing the images away. "That's it."

"Don't downplay what you experienced. That day was traumatic. Being in a similar situation and remembering what you saw in the last moments before losing part of your family had to be horrifying."

I nodded. Nausea churned in my stomach, and I pushed my plate away. I was done. I couldn't eat another bite, fearing I would throw it up.

"My brother, Chris, experienced amnesia when a mission went wrong. He had headaches if he tried to force the memories to return before his brain was ready. But they did come back. Maybe your mind is letting you know it's time to remember."

"Maybe. I'm not so sure."

"Go easy on yourself. The memories will come back when you're ready for them."

My stomach lurched, and fear danced along my spine. I didn't know why, but I was afraid he was right.

SIX

JULES

THE NEXT MORNING, CARL CALLED ME into his office for an update—not on my work, but on what was happening outside of the office, if anything. His large mahogany desk sat between us, overflowing with reports. I pushed the toe of my ballet flat against the back of the desk, simultaneously smoothing the flowered skirt that peeked through the buttons I'd left undone on my lab coat.

I should have worn the gray-and-black flowing skirt rather than the floral one. They were the same length and so very comfortable, but my mood called for darker colors that morning. It had not been in my closet. Maybe it was at the dry cleaner's. I could have sworn I'd picked it up, but maybe not.

Carl cleared his throat.

"I'm sorry, did you say something?"

"I asked if anything has happened outside of the office. Anything at all that you found unusual."

"Just a misplaced purse. It turned up in another room." I wouldn't be taken seriously by anyone at work about that. They knew me too well. Still, it had been on the table. I was sure of it. As for the missing skirt, I wasn't going to tell him as it was probably at the dry cleaner's. Same with a sweater I couldn't find. Besides, he suspected one of the soldiers I'd vaccinated, and I couldn't imagine what a guy would do with my skirt.

He waved it away. "That's not unusual, Jules."

Right, of course it wasn't. I scowled at him. "Don't you get a report from Trev? What's this really about?"

"Yes, I do. This is about keeping you safe if one of the soldiers has an unhealthy obsession with you. I also want to hear firsthand if you're worried about anything."

"I'm fine."

Carl ran his fingers through his short graying hair. "Good. Trev's team reported back about the soldiers from the first test group. They checked out." He leaned forward, and his features tightened. "I'm glad to hear about that, but you're going to have to put up with Trev guarding you for a while longer. I have a bad feeling, and it's better that we're proactive about your safety. With the disease threat in Russia, we'll need to add the building's surrounding area or lab onto his radar."

"We're helping. I doubt anyone from the Russian facility would be a threat. And they're not even here." I pushed to my feet. "Trev mentioned he teaches classes during the day. We're both busy, Carl. I'll be fine at work." There was nothing more to be said. After a few more words exchanged and wishing each other a good night, I headed down to the lobby, texting Trev as I went that I was ready to leave. His response was fast and curt: *Stay inside. Stuck in traffic—accident. Be there soon.*

I waved to the security guard at the front desk and leaned against the inside of one of the large glass panes in the front of the building. Restless, I scrolled through my contacts and hit the call button for my best friend, Becs, who'd also been my roommate in college.

"Hey, nerd," she said in greeting. "It's been over a week since you've called. I was getting worried."

I snorted. "Worried about what? That I'd gotten lost under a pile of research?" We were told to keep the information about the virus that had infected people in Russia contained and not to share anything outside our facility, which was hard because I wanted to talk to her about it. As a fellow scientist, I knew she would understand.

"That's what I was concerned about. You can go entirely too long without human interaction. What's up? Anything new?"

I chewed my bottom lip for a minute, contemplating. Becs and I told each other everything. "You heard about the scientist from our competitor who killed himself, right?" It had been a month before, but I couldn't get the incident out of my head.

"I did. So sad. Wait, did you know him?" Alarm colored her voice.

"Yes, but we weren't close. He was more of an acquaintance. We had talked about collaborating on a project that was giving both of us fits. Weird, I know, but he was a decent guy."

"Your bosses were okay with you teaming up with the competition?"

"Noooo." I laughed. "They didn't like the idea of working together at all. We convinced them we'd only be sharing a few notes and helping each other in the areas where we were stuck. They were against it until they figured out it could open up a whole new marketing strategy that would benefit both businesses."

"Always about the bottom line." Becs sighed.

"That wasn't what I wanted to tell you."

"No? There's more drama? Spill, girl."

I filled her in on the screen-saver incident, the missing purse, and falling overboard before finally getting to Trev.

Becs stopped me. "Let me get this straight. A man, who most of the women on your floor want, rescued you, and now he's in your life daily, guarding you?"

I laughed. "Yep. That's exactly right."

"Do you like him?"

I paused, nibbling on my lip some more. "He irritated me when I realized it was him. Becs, I don't know. There's more there than the man-candy he appears to be. When he held me on the boat, I felt safe. Protected. And there are moments where he lets me see into his past or drops his quick wit and charm to reveal so much more. Maybe I made too much of the flirting and lingering smiles between him and the flight attendant."

"Of course you did. I'm going to give you some advice, and I expect you to follow it."

I rolled my eyes even though she couldn't see me.

"Stop it." Becs laughed. "I know what you're doing."

"What are you talking about?" I was lucky to have her as my friend. She got me in ways that most didn't. We'd connected right away, even though we were complete opposites. Even at our mutual age of thirty, she was outgoing, and I was introverted. She was adventurous, and it reflected in her appearance—she had short blond hair that she styled to match her moods, spiky some days, sometimes soft waves, sometimes dyed outlandish colors. I was dark to her light—my olive complexion, long brown hair, and reserved disposition complementing both her look and her personality.

Becs cleared her throat, and I focused on our conversation.

"Forget that Trev initially came off as a flirt," she said. "He's not Brad. That was college, and that guy was a douche. Instead, focus on ending your extended stay in celibacy-land." Her voice softened. "This is good for you, Jules. Maybe not the weird stuff that's been happening, but you need to get back out there."

TREV

I HAD TO TEAR MY eyes from the window. Jules was in there, sitting at the kitchen table, drinking coffee, and reading a book. With a couple more twists, I finished tightening the last screw on the motion-sensor light by her back door.

Moving around, I triggered the light I'd just installed to

flood the back if anyone was outside. Tools in hand, I went inside. She looked up when I approached, and I grinned, trying to hide how the sight of her affected me. "I need your phone so I can install an app to view what the camera sees."

"Oh, that's convenient."

Our hands brushed against each other as I took her phone, making me even more aware of her than I already was. Concentrating on the screen, I downloaded the app and connected her account so that she could access the cameras. With her cell between us, I demonstrated what she needed to do.

"That's great." She grinned as my stomach growled.

"There's a restaurant on the beach not too far from here. Want to take a walk there, grab some dinner?"

She nodded. "Sure." She locked up behind us, and then we made our way down the path on the side of her house to the beach.

She dangled her sandals between her fingers as we walked along the shore while waves broke out of reach from us.

"So, Trev, when you aren't on babysitting duty, what do you like to do?"

"I'm guarding you, not babysitting."

She smiled, and I couldn't help but grin at her teasing.

"I like spending time with my family. We usually find ourselves in a mess of some sort, but it's nice when we hang out, grill, and drink some beers. Sometimes we go boating."

The moon shone down on us, and I caught her shudder.

"What made you uncomfortable? The boating comment?"

"Yeah, I'm not a huge fan of that… I don't mind boating, to be perfectly honest. It's being on the water if the weather is bad or there's a chance of a storm blowing in."

"Ah, the dunking you got from the race? Or your past?"

"Neither are good memories. Honestly, I'm not crazy about being on or in deep water. I'd rather not talk about that, though. Tell me about your family."

"You've met my brother, Chris. Then there are five other guys I grew up with who are more family to both of us than any blood relative ever was."

"That's a big group of guys. Do you see them often?"

"Yep. Our base is in Maine, where we get together the most. We expanded our group when we went into the military and added a few more to our team."

"Hmm. I wish I had something like that. My best friend and I work long hours and don't live very close. We can't get together as often as we'd like. You're lucky." I paused. "I was super close to my mom."

"It was just the two of you living here in the States? I'm not detecting an accent."

"Yes. We moved to the beach house when we came over from Italy. Her family was from there, but she was the last of them. As for the lack of accent, we spoke both Italian and English daily. In Italy we spoke English at home. When my mom and I moved here, we rarely spoke Italian, even at home.

"She passed away from ovarian cancer two years ago. There's not a day that goes by when I don't miss her. She was my biggest champion and best friend."

"I'm sorry. It must be hard for you."

She smiled, looking as if she was going to cry before a forced smile curled her lips. "I miss her. I have her cookbook. It's silly, but it's like she left little pieces of herself on the pages. When I cook, I can almost feel her at my side, guiding me."

"I'm glad you have that to remember her by." My stomach growled loudly, and I frowned. "You need to stop talking about food. I don't think my poor deprived stomach can take much more of it."

She laughed again, and I relaxed. A sad Jules was not good —she made me want to comfort her, and that was crossing a line.

"I'll cook for you, and I promise, no more talking about food." She winked, and I growled. She did that on purpose.

"You know, you possess a very dangerous weapon. You must be keeping your culinary skills hidden, or you'd have stalkers and marriage proposals by the dozens."

"Because the way to a man's heart is through his stomach?" She stubbed her toe on a shell and stumbled. I caught her elbow then slid my hand down, lacing our fingers together.

"That's one way." I couldn't help but tease her, and she jumped right in and played along. It was fun. My thumb brushed back and forth over the inside of her wrist. When I felt the raised skin, she paused, pulled up her sleeve, and showed me a long T-shaped scar.

"Before you ask, I don't remember anything about this. Must have happened when I was young."

I nodded, dropping the subject.

"Back to what we were talking about… Sadly, I don't have time for socializing. I usually run in the morning, go to work, eat, and then crash. Rinse and repeat."

I'd noticed that there weren't any pictures of her family in her home except for a few of her and her mom. "What about going out with friends? You don't work every weekend."

"When I'm not working more than five days in a row, I'll get together with my friend Becs from college, but that's usually for a longer weekend. Or Fran and I will grab a drink or dinner after work sometimes."

"And Fran is?"

"My assistant. The one I walked out with the other day."

"Right, the one who called you Brainy. Does that make her Pinky?"

"What?"

I turned to her in shock. "You mean to tell me you never watched *Pinky and the Brain*?" She shook her head, and I laughed. "You're missing out. We'll have to watch an episode some night. The Brain is all about world domination."

We made our way up the wooden planks to Seaside Grill and placed our orders at the take-out window.

"Becs comes and visits when she can, but she lives over an hour away. We talk on the phone once or twice a week."

"What does she do?"

"She's a scientist like me and has similar hours."

Our food came up, and we grabbed our trays. Food in hand, we found seats. I bit into my cheeseburger and groaned. God, I was hungry.

She held a fry delicately between her fingers, pausing halfway to her mouth. "This is almost like a date." Her face went beet red.

I grinned. She was sexy, and I was going to cross that line with her eventually. I wondered whether she was after a date—I had no problem with that. "Would it be so bad"—I leaned across the table and tucked a piece of her hair behind her ear—"to go on a date with me?"

SEVEN

IT WAS LATE AFTERNOON, AND the happiness from spending time with Trev the night before had shifted to confusion and outright irritation. My day needed a do-over already. My head was pounding as I listened to my assistant. Fran stood in front of me and swore I'd told her to do something that I had not: "You told me to add in tea tree right after lunch."

I threw up my hands in frustration. "There is no way I would have said that. It would have compromised the integrity of the baseline experiment. The tea tree was for the second strand, which we already cultured. Seriously, you know that." With twenty percent of our time spent on our other projects, we had switched from studying the viral strains of the ancient hemorrhagic fever to the healing salve we were manipulating for military use.

We were testing lavender oil to speed tissue regeneration and increase collagen to decrease healing time. The second batch had various herbs, like tea tree oil, which we hoped would help to combat bacteria. We tested them separately in combination with key ingredients to speed regeneration by seventy-five percent over traditional methods.

"I know, but you said"—she made air quotes and mimicked the snotty face I made when I was frustrated with people not understanding—"'just do it. Don't question me.'"

Shoot, that was a pretty good impression. Still, what the hell? "Are you sick? Or high?"

Fran's lips peeled back, and she practically growled, "Are we done for the day? I've got an awful headache."

Make that two of us. "Yeah, go home and get some rest." I needed to let it go. She looked terrible. A sliver of worry shot through me that somehow the virus had infected her, but there was no way. When we worked on the strains from Russia, we wore biohazard suits and conducted the experiments in containment rooms. "Feel better, Franny."

I dropped onto my chair. She yanked her purse out of her desk drawer then stomped out of the office. With a glance around the lab, I gave the scientists who had enjoyed the show the evil eye. *What the hell is going on today?*

I picked up the platform of test tubes that contained the mixtures we were developing to increase the process of healing from injury. As I walked slowly to the secure chiller, I couldn't make sense of what had happened or of the fact that Fran had left before making sure our work was put away, safe from my klutziness.

After sending Trev a quick text saying I was done for the day, I got my purse from the drawer and headed out. I passed through the security door to our lab, rode the elevator down, and said good night to the evening guard. The sounds of the city blasted my senses as soon as I was on the sidewalk. I wanted to go home and was relieved to see Trev waiting for me, leaning against his car with his arms crossed over his broad chest.

I gazed at him in appreciation before I passed through the doorway—even though I was tired, I could enjoy the picture he presented. I could get used to him, if only the reason he was waiting for me was real rather than a job.

Neither of us spoke on the ride home. Trev probably sensed my mood was not good. After unlocking the door and going inside, I went right to the kitchen and grabbed a bottle of wine and a glass. Looking over my shoulder, I lifted my eyebrows and held up the glass. At his nod, I snagged a second, and we filed out to the patio. A mild breeze swept my hair back from my face. Trev took the bottle and corkscrew from me. In a matter of seconds, I was sipping a much-needed drink. I sank fully into the chair and lifted my feet onto the seat next to me while he settled in a few inches away.

Minutes passed while we enjoyed the wine and listened to the crash of the waves not far from my house. I loved it there—it was truly peaceful. I twisted the glass around by the stem, and spidery legs swirled at the edges. I had half a glass before I relaxed a bit.

He must have had a sixth sense or something. "What happened today?" he asked, his deep voice tempting me to confide in him

I turned to face him. Leaning over, I brushed a spider from his shoulder.

He cringed. "Was it a spider?"

Giddiness bubbled in my chest. "Don't tell me you're afraid of spiders?"

"Like you're not? All those legs and creepy eyes."

"I'm a scientist, so no." I laughed. "I can't believe you, a former Navy SEAL, are squeamish about a tiny arachnid."

He scowled at me. "Yeah well, it's something that lives in the back of my mind. It hasn't been easy. Imagine being in the field, unable to move, while one crawls across your forearm or even worse, your face."

The faraway look haunting his deep-blue eyes caused my chest to tighten around my heart. His answer didn't ring true. "I'm not following your reasoning. You're a pretty tough guy. What brought about a fear of spiders?"

He leaned back in his chair so its weight shifted onto the back legs. If I hadn't been trying to get him to open up, I might have nudged him and played with his precarious balancing act.

He rocked his chair back onto four legs and placed his wineglass on the table between us. "When you grow up in a home overrun with filth, insects, and vermin, it leaves a lasting impression. I didn't like living like that, and I guess the feeling of all those legs crawling on me brings me back to when I didn't have options for escaping that existence."

I ducked my head to hide my emotions. I'd seriously misjudged him. "I'm sorry."

"Why would you be sorry? You weren't my keeper when I was growing up."

Keeper? That's an odd way for him to think of his parents. Maybe he didn't grow up with them. "I had you pegged all wrong. I assumed you were mostly fluff—you know, without substance."

"Ah, the surfer vibe." He laughed. "Appearances are deceiving."

"I did think of you as a beach bum. You have that look." His blond man bun, athletic body, bright smile and eyes, and the easy way he carried himself added up to make it seem as if he didn't take himself seriously.

"And you thought of me as a player."

"Well, come on! Look at you." I grinned. "And there was the flirting you did on the plane."

He shot me a confused look.

"The flight attendant."

"Jess? She's a friend, and I was giving her a hard time about her boyfriend."

"Oh, I'm sorry. My mistake. It was her reaction, the blushing." I waved at my face. "And then you turned that charm on me." *This is embarrassing.* "But the spider... I didn't think much could bother you."

He wrapped an arm around me and gave me a quick squeeze before he moved back into his space. "Someone had to be lighthearted. I don't think we would have survived our youth if I hadn't taken on that role. My brother is the serious one."

"Chris?"

He nodded, his gaze turning inward, distant. "He shouldered the brunt of everything while we were growing up. It was my way of helping him to bring laughter back and lighten up the situation we were in. I wanted to take some of the responsibility off him, to shield him like he'd done so many times for me when I was much younger."

My curiosity was a dangerous thing with a will of its own. "Was this while you were growing up with your parents?" It sounded like foster care gone wrong, but there were a lot of parents out there who weren't protective and loving with their kids. I was grateful for mine, or at least the one I could remember. She was one of the best a kid could have had.

"Yes, we lived with our mom and dad until she died." He got a faraway look in his eyes. "It wasn't all bad even after that. We had somewhere to go in high school on occasion, and then after, we had a place. We lived with our friends—we saved each other, our sanity, and survived to get out of that hellhole. Those were the guys who became a real family to Chris and me." There was a tightness bracketing his mouth, carving lines that weren't usually there.

"Is that why you're teaching women's self-defense?"

He looked surprised.

"Carl told me."

He nodded. "It is. My mom gave up. If I can help one woman get out of a bad situation, it eases some of my memories."

There was so much more to him than I'd thought. I was embarrassed by how I'd judged him on appearance and from a brief encounter between him and the flight attendant.

I could share some vulnerability about myself. It didn't compare to his, but it was something. He had demons in his closet, too, and he'd shown some of them to me, so the least I could do the same. "I'm terrified of being in the deep water when it's storming, alone and drowning."

He leaned forward, enveloped one of my hands with his large one, and gave mine a gentle squeeze before he released me.

I wanted more. I wanted to turn my palm up so that our hands clasped. He made things easier, somehow. I understood the gift he'd given his brother. He drew the darkness away so light could shine once more.

He smiled gently. "Traumatic experiences do that, but in time, I think you'll overcome those fears enough to enjoy being on the water in iffy weather."

"Maybe. I've had years of counseling, so I manage. Running helps me process when too much is going on in my head or my anxiety starts to choke me."

"You haven't been jogging lately, have you?" He leaned back in his chair again, his intense blue eyes capturing and holding me hostage.

"No. I've been either exhausted and sleeping in until the last possible second, or…" I didn't want to say it, but I felt like I was being watched. Running in the early morning, sometimes before the sun came up, didn't seem like the smartest thing to do for the time being. The memory void from my accident made me vulnerable as it was, and inviting him into my head added to the paranoia about being watched. I needed more time to get to know him better before I could trust he wouldn't think I was crazy.

Silence stretched between us, and I suddenly felt like I was one of the samples I studied under a microscope. *Can he see my concerns? Did I give too much away?*

"Carl shared with me what you're working on for the Russian research facility. While I agree with him that it's a long shot that the threat is coming from them, I'll check out everyone associated with the people who were infected."

I nodded. I didn't want to talk about it. I wondered whether I would have been able to save them if they'd had access to the delta-32 mutation I was perfecting. "All I've been doing lately is worrying. The testing we're doing is constantly on my mind."

"Why don't I come by early tomorrow, and we can run together?"

I could really use that. It'll take the edge off my overactive imagination and maybe eliminate the added stress. This is good. Safe. And I don't have to confess any silly fears about perceived noises or writing that isn't there, which is making me feel weak. "You think you can keep up with me?"

A wicked grin spread across his face, and his eyes danced with mirth. "You challenging me, Brainy?"

I was never going to live that one down. "Just stating a fact. I ran a marathon recently." He was a *former* Navy SEAL. *How much competition could he be?*

"Game on." With a foot on the table's rim, he balanced on his tilted chair. "Why don't we raise the stakes? If I win, I take you to dinner this weekend."

Warmth trickled through me, and my smile spread from ear to ear. I couldn't help it. I liked him. He was so much more than the first impression I'd gotten before the boating incident. "As a date?"

"You bet, Sweet Cheeks."

I did laugh that time. "Really? That's the term you're going with?" I took another sip of my wine. "If you think you stand a chance of winning… I'm all in. What do I get if I win?"

"Anything you want. I'll even let you name your prize after the race."

"You're on." It was going to be fun. I needed to figure out what I wanted more than a date. Because if I was honest with myself, I wanted that too.

We gathered the empty bottle of wine and the glasses then headed inside. After making sure the back door was locked the and shades were drawn, he took his leave—that was, once he heard the lock click on the front door behind him, which I knew from shamelessly standing by the door with my palm against the wood.

I still felt warm inside, which I could have chalked up to the two glasses of wine I'd consumed, but I suspected it was from him. With a smile curving my lips, I shut the lights off as I made my way to my bedroom to get ready for bed. I pulled open the drawer on my dresser to take out a tank top and loose pajama pants but then froze. On the dresser, where it always sat, was a picture taken a few years ago of my mom and me. A very light coating of dust covered the top of the furniture, except for a thin line where the picture had been. It had been moved.

I rubbed my face with my hands, my anxiety climbing as I debated contacting Trev. Several minutes passed until I made myself brush my teeth and change into clothes to sleep. I climbed into bed. There had to be an explanation.

Or at least that's what I tried to convince myself as I tossed and turned, while the sheets morphed into a boa constrictor from my movements. Morning was a long way away.

EIGHT

Y LEGS ACHED AS I pushed open the door to the building I worked in. Even though I was sore from the race with Trev that morning, it had been invigorating. He'd won, and anticipation about what that meant buzzed through me—we would be going on a date.

I flashed my badge at Josh, the security guard, before swiping it.

He grinned. "Back already?"

My feet slowed as I raised my eyebrows. *Right, because I'm a workaholic with no life outside the lab.* My colleagues teased me about it even though most of them were the same way. So yes, of course, I was back again. "Yep. I can't seem to stay away. Those pesky little technicalities like needing a paycheck come into play."

He didn't smile or laugh as I thought he would.

I opened my mouth to question him, but then several people entered, and he turned his attention to them. Shrugging, I let it go.

When I got to my desk and dropped my purse in a drawer, I heard my name. I looked up to Carl leaning into the lab's entrance. He waved me to his office.

I crossed to his large office, with its panoramic view of skyscrapers and peeks of the ocean in between. I took a seat in front of him. "Morning, Carl."

"Jules"—he dragged his hand across his forehead and

flinched. A pained expression briefly crossed his features—"I don't even know how to tell you this."

Alarm raced through me. "Just say it, whatever it is."

"This isn't public knowledge, at least not yet." He rubbed his face again before meeting my gaze. "Fran was found in her apartment this morning by a neighbor. They had a standing routine to exercise in the morning. When Fran missed then didn't answer her door or phone, the neighbor let herself in."

"Is she okay?" Panic shot down my arms, making my fingers tingle. *The virus.* "Was it—"

"No, she hadn't been infected by the virus, but I'm sorry to tell you that she isn't okay. Fran's dead, Jules. There was no sign of forced entry, no defensive wounds. It was ruled a suicide."

"What? How?" My brain was spinning. Fran hadn't seemed depressed. She'd looked so run-down the day before, and that fight we had—the last words we'd spoken to each other weren't the best. I felt terrible.

"I don't have any more details than that. I'm sorry, Jules. She'll be missed."

"I—" Tremors ran through my hands, and I clasped them in my lap, trying to control it. I didn't understand how she could be gone. "Is there going to be an investigation? I mean, come on, Carl, you know Fran. She wasn't depressed. There's no way she would have harmed herself."

He shook his head. "It's hard to tell what's going on in people's heads. Sometimes pain can be hidden until no one is around. That's when they're most vulnerable to things that happened during the day, how they're feeling…"

No… Does he think she killed herself because of the fight we had? Does everyone think that? My stomach cramped, and I fought down the bile that was climbing my throat. I didn't want to face anyone.

"We'll know more after the coroner's and medical examiner's reports. I know you were close. Go home. Take the day off. I've already called Trev to come to pick you up."

I numbly got my things and made my way to the elevator. My mind spun—I didn't understand how she could have done it. Tears flooded my eyes as I stepped off the elevator and exited the building. Instead of standing by the doors and waiting for Trev, I pivoted on a heel and walked, head down, toward the ocean. People weaved out of my way. I did not. Several shoulders bumped against mine, dislodging more tears, but I didn't care.

I should have paid attention.

TREV

THE DRIVER OF THE CAR in front of me was taking his sweet time putting his damn foot on the accelerator once the light changed. I impatiently inched forward. I tapped Jules's number on my phone and spoke through the speakers in the car when she answered. "I'm on my way. Hang in there."

She said "okay" in a shaky voice then disconnected the call. My instincts screamed that something was going on. I needed details to fit the puzzle pieces together before anyone else got hurt.

I called Chris and waited for him to pick up the phone. He finally grumbled a groggy hello.

"You busy?" I clipped out.

"I was, but not anymore. What do you want?"

I filled him in on the latest with Jules's case. "I need more information than 'suicide.'"

"I'd say so." Chris yawned. "Lots of weird stuff happening around that woman."

"Right, so can you dig up the details?"

"Yeah. Mari is doing something with the girls today—"

"Hannah and Liv?"

"Yes. They're having a girls' morning or something like that. Liv won an award for one of her sculptures and sold it for a few thousand, so they're celebrating. Liam, Jack, and I stayed behind—because we weren't invited—to get some work done."

"Congrats to Liv. Let her know I said that, okay?"

Chris said he would.

"Jack would be a big help on this too."

"You think I can't hack into the California police servers?"

I had to poke the bear. He made it too easy. "I have my doubts. If Jack can't do it, he has Hannah, and she's badass. No offense, bro. You're good, but that team is lethal."

"Next time I see you, I'm kicking your ass." The line went dead, and I burst out laughing. I loved my brother, but opportunities to challenge him were too good to pass up. I knew he would get the information I needed and then some. If he ran into a block, which he wouldn't, as his hacking skills were better than Jack's, he would find another way. He always did.

My grin fell as I pulled up to find that Jules wasn't waiting for me behind the glass panes of her office building. I searched along the sidewalk until I saw a glimpse of her walking with her head down, clearly not paying attention.

A man moved along the crowded sidewalk behind her. The hood of his sweatshirt was up, obscuring any view of his face. I didn't like it. *Fuck.* I jolted the vehicle forward, slammed on the brakes, then jumped out. He was inches from her. In the next second, I lost her.

A woman cried out.

"Hey!" I yelled, shoving through people to get to her.

She was on the sidewalk. The man who'd pushed her down was nowhere to be seen. I lifted her up, scanning the area. Half a block away, I caught a glimpse of him as he rounded the corner on a black crotch rocket. Goddamn, I wanted to go after him, but she was my priority. "Are you hurt?"

"Ah, no." She brushed her scraped palms on her pants.

She pushed her sunglasses up on her nose before she

turned to me, but it didn't stop me from seeing the tear tracks on her cheeks.

"Are you sure?" I ran my hands up and down her arms.

She gave me a small nod. "Can we go? I want to go home." Her hands trembled.

Shit. I need to get more guys out here or at least extend our perimeter to include her office building. With my arm around her shoulders, I led her to the car and got her settled before going around to my side. I didn't miss the way she leaned into me. I decided to give her a few minutes to process what had happened before I questioned her.

I eased back into traffic. Neither of us said a word. I didn't give her long. "Did you see who that man was? Did he say anything to you?"

"No. He grabbed me. You yelled. Then he shoved me to the ground. I didn't hear his voice. But…"

"What?" I shifted my gaze from the road for a moment.

Her words were quiet and measured. She kept her gaze locked on her hands. "I caught a faint whiff of peppermint. Maybe gum? I don't know. It could have been some on the sidewalk."

It could've been. "It's better to note anything you observed in case it ties to that man." I didn't say it to her, but he had been tall and lean, agile in the way he moved. There was a good chance he was part of one of her military groups, but my gut still said that was the wrong angle. Why, I wasn't sure, but we would figure it out.

When I pulled up in front of her house, she turned to me, her lower lip trembling. "Thanks for the ride." She was out the door in a flash.

"Do you want me to come in?"

"I appreciate it, but no. I want to be alone."

I let her go against my better judgment. The guy shoving her must have rattled her, but probably not as badly as the news about her assistant. Once she was safely inside, I went to the police station to see what information I could get about Fran. I would go back and check on Jules later. For the time being, she probably wanted to cry without an audience. That was my guess. Death sucked. It was a giant sucker punch that I was sure had shaken her world.

Even though my parents had been horrible to Chris and me, our mom's death had been a blow we weren't expecting. Lucky for us, we had a great support system in place with our crew. Those memories of our parents were from a long time ago.

I shook it off. I needed answers. Halfway to the police station, my cell rang. I hit the button on the steering wheel to connect the call via Bluetooth.

Chris's voice boomed through the speakers and filled the interior of my SUV. "I was able to get past their passwords and into the main police database. The reports aren't complete, but I found some strange notes about the case."

"Well?" If Fran's death wasn't a suicide, Jules was in way more trouble than we'd thought.

"There were two incisions on her arm. One cut along her forearm and followed the radial artery, and then a separate incision bisected horizontally through both the radial and ulnar arteries at the wrist. They both formed a T."

Like the scar Jules had. "Fran was a scientist, so the precision makes sense, but it seems like overkill for a suicide." That was a bad choice of words, but I couldn't figure out why Fran had cut herself to match Jules's scar. Carl had told me about the office disagreement, but something didn't add up. I puffed out a breath. "No sign of forced entry or a struggle?"

"No, nothing like that, but there was something else. The cord to her alarm clock was lying over her palm. The time had stopped at 7:16 a.m. Does that mean anything to you?"

"Not a thing, but it seems like it should." I scratched the stubble along my jaw, wondering what we were missing.

"I cross-checked Jules's mom's time of death. It was in the

afternoon. They'll do an autopsy as well as find out whose fingerprints are on the knife. There are empty bottles of alcohol in the garbage. Some of the evidence points to depression."

Still, the scar sat wrong. It felt like a message, a personal one. I told Chris about the similar marks. Silence stretched between us as I weighed my options. "I've got a bad feeling about this but can't quite put my finger on why, or if there is foul play, or from where."

"Yeah, I agree. We've got the boating accident, the weird screen-saver note, then the assistant dying. And on top of that, she's working to find a solution to help people in Russia who came into contact with an ancient virus. Something isn't adding up." He waited for a beat. "Is there a chance Jules killed her?"

"No. I can't even imagine that."

Chris snorted. "I talked with Connor earlier. He thinks you're personally involved."

"I'm not even going to dignify that with an answer." I'd pulled Connor, one of the members of our team, onto the job to help with security around Jules's house. He was overstepping with his assumptions and stirring up trouble for me with the guys.

"It's my job to look out for you, Trev. If I find out there's anything wrong or mentally unstable with this chick, you damn well better believe I'll be there in a second. I've got your back, always."

I couldn't be objective where she was concerned. I loved my brother more than anything, but the shit with Jules— dammit, I had crossed a line. I cared too much. "Who's in Maine right now besides you and Mari?"

"Liam, Liv, Jack, and Hannah. Why? Are you thinking of bringing Jules here?"

Maybe it was time to let the team do an evaluation with unbiased eyes. "I am. The funeral is on Sunday, so I've got the weekend for you guys to help me poke around and see if there's anything I'm missing."

"Good. I want to check her out too. Or better yet, have Hannah do it. Since espionage is her thing, she should be able to tell if Jules is hiding anything."

It was definitely her thing. Raised as a spy for Russia, she was trained for interrogation and mental and physical torture, which our government also liked to utilize to ferret out deception.

"I don't think she's purposely hiding something," I said. "But there could be some piece of information she doesn't think connects. I need the girls to see if they can get anything out of her. I'd think her guard would drop some around them, at least with Liv."

"Seriously? You're throwing Mari under the bus?"

"It's not like that, but she's a ballbuster, and Hannah can be downright scary. You know what I mean."

Chris snorted. "Whatever, man. When will we see you?"

"Late Friday night. We'll get in, and she'll probably crash soon after that. We'll have all day Saturday to try to get what we need out of this messed-up situation."

NINE

O NCE EVERYONE WHO NEEDED TO be present was seated in Carl's office, he connected via video chat to Dr. Andrei Mikhailov and his team in Russia to discuss the death of their field scientist, Sasha. Maybe sixty years in age, Andrei appeared fragile with a hawklike nose and thinning gray hair. Wire spectacles perched on his nose, but his dark-brown eyes were warm as he greeted us. I forced a small smile in return. Carl led the discussion while I willed my tense muscles to relax.

"Our findings concur with the ones you've reported, Andrei. The virus is lethal and ancient in origin. We haven't seen it before, but it mimics some of the worst aspects of Marburg hemorrhagic fever. Have you determined how the infection spread to Sasha and if anyone else is at risk?"

The first viral hemorrhagic-fever outbreak that we knew of dated back to the 1700s. The virus gained access to the immune system through CCR5, a gene responsible for the production of a protein. Many scientific hypotheses suggested that the delta-32 mutation came about as a natural genetic defense due to such outbreaks as the lethal fevers. Those who had the CCR5-delta-32 mutation survived the epidemics.

I happened to agree with the hemorrhagic theory, and that's why I'd done extensive research into how to implant the genetic wonder into those who did not have it. My research used CCR5-delta-32 as the key to combat entrance for many diseases and viruses that attempted to gain a toehold in the immune system.

Andrei cleared his throat. "We found a family who died in the same manner as Sasha. Her colleagues on-site said she knew the husband and wife and had gone a day early to visit before the rest of the team arrived. Our best guess is she drank some of their water, which was contaminated due to melting permafrost around the burial site."

"Have the residents been evacuated?" Carl asked.

"They have and are in quarantine until we are positive they do not have the virus," Andrei confirmed. "So far, it seems very localized to that family, as their closest neighbor was one hundred fifty kilometers away."

Carl turned to me, and his facial expression suggested an invitation to reveal my findings.

"We've sent over a batch of antibodies that have been shown to be effective against similar viruses. During our preliminary testing, the fever slowed once the antibodies were introduced, and some even halted the illness's progress. While it's not a hundred percent, at least there is a chance of survival."

"Thank you, my dear," Andrei said to me before turning his focus back to Carl. "And the delta-32 injections your facility has created? What about those? It would help ensure that the rest of us have another level of protection against other threats buried in the permafrost."

Excited murmurs from his team and shocked ones from ours confused the communication. My gaze shot to Carl. The injections weren't public knowledge. Somehow, we had a serious leak.

I SETTLED BACK INTO MY airplane seat—Trev was flying us

to Maine. He hadn't given me a choice. When he picked me up for work, he made sure I had packed a bag for the weekend. Honestly, if I hadn't gone with him, I would have spent my entire Saturday in bed.

I hadn't said it, but I was really glad we were getting away. Work was difficult and depressing without Fran there. I poured everything I had into my job, knowing a breakthrough was near, but it wasn't the same without Fran's teasing and refusing to let me carry anything. She always said I was a menace to experiments with my inability to walk gracefully from one end of the office to the other without stumbling or bumping into a chair or desk.

I swiped tears from my face. Nothing would be the same without her there.

In what felt like no time at all, we landed, and after we taxied to a hangar, Trev escorted me to a Jeep.

"We're really staying on a wild blueberry farm?" When he'd told me, I couldn't quite believe it. But it sounded peaceful, so I went with it. The distraction would help because Sunday would suck.

It was dark out by the time we pulled to a stop in front of a gorgeous house. Waves crashed in the distance. I'd caught sight of a sign as we drove under it. "You didn't say this was also a winery." I could use some wine.

Trev put the Jeep in Park and walked around to my side as I stepped onto the circular driveway. "The farm grows wild blueberries and hybrid grapes. I'm sure you'll enjoy the wine."

"I bet I will. A glass right about now would be very welcome."

We followed the walkway to the house, and Trev pounded on the door. I crossed my arms over my stomach. *I shouldn't be here. Why hadn't I insisted on going to Becs's house for the weekend?* That would've been preferable to having to pretend I was okay in front of a bunch of strangers, even if they were family to Trev.

He smiled down at me, unraveled my arms, and clasped my hand as the door opened. The warmth of his hand seeped into my chilled fingers. Maybe being with him for the weekend was the best option, after all. I leaned into him and decided to make the most of the next twenty-four hours.

A woman with mahogany hair and a warm smile held the door open. I offered her a closed-lipped smile, too exhausted to infuse any life in my expression as I entered. She looked Italian with her cognac eyes, classic features, and olive-toned skin. After Trev came inside, she wrapped her arms around me in a quick hug, whispering, "I'm so sorry about your friend, Jules."

I fought the tears that flooded my eyes. It took a few blinks. "Thank you for having me."

"You're very welcome. I'm Liv, and we're so happy you're here. Let me introduce you to everyone and then show you where you'll be staying."

Trev took my bag from my hands, and I followed Liv to a large room in the back of the house with a fireplace and access to the backyard patio. I recognized Chris from the boating mishap right away. His arm was wrapped around a woman with long hair a similar shade to Liv's, if not a tad darker. Liv made introductions. Mari stepped forward and squeezed my hands, repeating the same thing Liv had said about Fran.

I kept a tight grip on my emotions and said hello to the other man, Liv's husband, Liam. He had stunning green eyes and traces of a dreamy Irish brogue. I stifled a yawn.

Liv must have taken pity on me. "You look tired, Jules. I'll show you where you're sleeping."

"Want me to come with?" Trev asked as I walked by him.

"No. I'll be fine. I'm going to pass out as soon as my head hits the pillow."

"I'll be close by if you need anything."

I almost threw myself into his arms at the warmth emanating from his gaze. I nodded, unable to trust my words at this point. Liv led me to my room and opened the door.

"There are towels in the bathroom, and if you need anything at all let any one of us know."

"I appreciate it." After she left, I made quick work of getting ready for sleep. As I climbed into bed, I welcomed the numbness that stole over me, allowing my mind to quiet enough so that I would be able to pass out without nonstop anguish over Fran. Tomorrow would be a new day, and with it would come a houseful of people I didn't really know.

TEN

A KNOCK SOUNDED AT MY door, jolting me awake. *Where am I?* As I blinked the world into focus, I took in the room where I'd awakened. I was in a large bed, bigger than mine at home, with a fluffy white duvet. The room was painted in a soft grayish purple. It was soothing and pretty, but when reality crashed back into me, tears welled. Fran was gone, and her absence was a hole in my heart.

"Get your running clothes on and meet me downstairs."

I swiped at the corners of my eyes and managed a half smile or maybe a grimace at Trev's muffled demand through my closed door, pushing off the cloud of grief I'd been blanketed in since Fran's death. *He's good for me.*

Trev wanted to go for a run, and I was game. Last time, he'd beaten me, but I was determined that the next win would be mine. I shoved off the covers and yelled for him to give me five minutes. My hand curled around my cell phone. There were two messages from Becs. One asked where the hell I was. The second asked how was I doing. I let her know I was in Maine for the weekend and that I was doing as well as could be expected.

Cloying sadness inched over the spark of happiness Trev had instilled when he'd awakened me, but I wouldn't let it win. I missed Fran, and nothing would change that, but I was determined to be good company while I was a guest there.

I threw on shorts and a long-sleeved shirt then quickly

brushed my teeth and pulled my hair into a ponytail before heading downstairs to meet him. Running would take my mind off things I didn't want to think about. I needed it.

Mari was sitting at the table when I entered the kitchen. With a big cup of coffee in her hands, she offered a sleepy smile. "Going out?"

I opened my mouth to answer, but Trev beat me to it. "Running." He pointed to her. "Don't make breakfast. Tell Liv too. Loser has to cook." He turned to me and grinned. "My money is on Sweet Cheeks."

What the hell? What era are we in? I marched right over to him, grabbed his shirt, and yanked him to eye level. Before he could pull away, I snarled, "Wrong century."

Mari spewed coffee over the table as she burst out laughing. "That'll teach you. Don't mess with a woman who hasn't had her coffee."

"Isn't that the truth?" I winked. Mari was obviously tough and didn't take anyone's crap, and she seemed genuine in her defense of me. It was easy to remember who was who after meeting them last night. They were very different.

"I knew there was a reason I liked you." Mari grinned before getting up and refilling her mug. "I'll let everyone know you'll be cooking, Trev."

"Where's the loyalty, Mari?" He shook his head and tried to look disappointed. The mirth dancing in his eyes contrasted with his words and actions. "I'm going to have to speak to my brother about getting you back in line."

Mari plucked a knife from the wooden block and leaned against the counter. With coffee in one hand, she tossed the blade into the air then caught it by the handle. "I'd like to see you both try."

I shifted from one foot to another, wondering what kind of family theirs was.

"Morning." Liv walked in, took one look at Mari, then glared at Trev. "What did you do?"

"Nothing, I swear." Laughing, Trev grabbed my hand and pulled me to the door leading from the kitchen.

"If she cooks, we're cooking with her!" Mari yelled after us.

My brain didn't want to process what had happened in there, so I quietly stretched alongside Trev. It was chilly outside, much more so than fall mornings in California. I shivered despite my long-sleeved shirt. After a few minutes, he offered a hand to help me up. Fog was lifting off the ground, and the crisp pine-scented air enticed me to take a deep breath.

"Ready?"

"Where are we running?"

"We'll follow the driveway out and run along the road until we see a path on the right."

I nodded, and we took off slowly at first, letting our muscles warm up. It didn't take long before both of us lengthened our strides. It was beautiful there—I could get used to it. I let my mind wander while I matched pace as best as I could to Trev's longer stride.

The trail was amazing. We ran beneath a canopy of trees and caught glimpses of the ocean through the branches. The rolling waves sounded like the ocean did at home and helped to settle me. It was peaceful. Even so, I couldn't shake the sadness of Fran's tragedy that clung to my soul. I missed her. Tears intermingled with the sweat that ran down my face, but I didn't care.

After we turned and headed back, we kept the same pace. It was nice, and I wasn't opposed to running with Trev at all. He pushed me in more ways than one, out of my comfort zone and letting someone new in. Whatever was going on at work or with the odd things at home, at least I had a friendship with him. It surprised me. I never thought we would have become friends, not after the way a couple of the women in my office had behaved when he was around. That had felt like high school all over again, and that wasn't something I wanted to repeat.

As we got closer, we both increased our speed. There was no way I would beat him, in spite of my long legs.

He flew in front of me, and I put on as much speed as I could. We were using the sign over the beginning of the driveway as the finish line. Gasping for breath, I slowed as soon as I crossed. Trev was way ahead of me.

Jogging backward, he grinned. "What's for breakfast, beautiful?"

I almost tripped. *Beautiful? He must've been joking.* I flipped him off then plopped down in the grass, waiting for my breath to even out before I loosened my muscles.

Beside me, Trev stretched his hamstrings and hip flexors. I had to force myself to ignore the way his shirt clung to him. A drop of sweat trailed along his cheek, dangled from his chin, then fell to his washboard abs. My stomach clenched. He was in great shape, with well-defined muscles. When he moved, his muscles rippled, and I wanted to run my hands from his chiseled face, down his corded neck, and along his rock-hard chest. Shaking my head, I pushed to my feet. "See you inside. I'm showering before breakfast."

Keeping my back ramrod straight, I fought the urge to look over my shoulder to see if he was watching me walk in the house. Not even a second later, I felt him behind me. The heat of him was close, and every inch of me tingled. I wanted him to crowd me so I could feel his body against mine. We stepped into the kitchen together, and as he passed me, his fingers trailed across the back of my thigh. I bit back a moan as my heart raced and my knees threatened to buckle.

On wobbly legs, I made my way to my borrowed room and the shower. My reaction to him wasn't supposed to happen. It never had with anyone else before, not like that. Sure, I'd had boyfriends, but they were comfortable, our intimacy enjoyable. Trev was different. His touch was combustible.

I got ready quickly and found myself back in the kitchen where Mari, Liv, and a tall blond woman with crystalline eyes was standing. She was stunning and frightening at the same time. I tucked my hair behind my ears, suddenly nervous.

"Don't let her make you uncomfortable. Hannah has this ice-queen thing she does." Mari jumped from her seat and went to the fridge. "What are we making? I'm starving."

Hannah's lips twitched before she turned on her heel and left, muttering something about not cooking.

"Italian baked eggs and sausage." Distracted, I said the first thing that came to mind.

"Oh, Italian food." Liv rubbed her palms together. "That sounds amazing."

"I'm at a loss. You'll have to tell us what to do." Mari shrugged.

"I'm sorry to hear about your friend's passing." Liv squeezed my arm.

I blinked away tears. My heart was heavy, but Fran would have loved a morning like mine. It was easy for me to think of her there, enjoying herself. Mari wrapped her arms around me for a quick hug. I murmured my thanks, and they must have sensed I didn't want to talk about how much I missed her in that moment, because neither woman said anything more about it.

Liv reached around me, took out the eggs, and set them on the counter. "How did you meet Trev?"

I snuck a peck at her from beneath my lashes. Beside them, I felt self-conscious. Not being in my element and among Trev's family was different from cooking at home.

Needing a few things from the fridge, I veered around Mari but stumbled over her foot, or maybe my own. Her hand shot out and caught my elbow. Saved from a face-plant, I flashed her a wobbly smile.

I rummaged through the fridge and pulled out what I needed. Tomatoes sat on the counter—they would need to be roasted. I busied myself by prepping them before starting the sausage on the stove. "He flew my boss and me to DC a few times. Aside from that, I didn't really know him."

Liv nudged my shoulder. "There's more to the story. Don't hold out on us."

Is there? No. Not in the way Liv was suggesting. I shrugged. "He's sort of babysitting me."

"What?" Mari burst out laughing. "This is gold. Tell us. I want something to tease him about."

Liv took over cooking the sausage.

"Is it possible to faze him?" Their warmth was infectious, and I couldn't resist learning anything about him outside of what I already knew. "He's so easy to be around, most of the time."

Liv shrugged. "There are things that get under his skin, but he's a good guy. Mari likes giving him a hard time because he doesn't take himself seriously. He's fun."

"Yeah, he is." That was something I needed more of: fun. And him. I wanted him, and my eyes widened as I realized that I liked him that way. I hid my emotions by yanking the bowl over and cracking the eggs in a one-handed flurry.

"I see you've done this before." Mari moved closer. "Tell us what to do next to help while you fill us in about the situation with you and Trev."

"Yes, do," Liv chimed in.

Liv's voice was casual, but I wasn't buying it. Maybe she was protective of the family. I gave them each a task with the food that was already out on the counter before I answered the questions they kept asking. "Trev started to guard me after I fell overboard in California. We were on my boss's boat, racing another company. I lost my footing and went over the rail. Trev saved me."

Liv set the knife down and gave me her full attention. Mari did, too, and reached out to grab my wrist. "He saved you?"

Liv grinned. "Would you expect anything less from one of our guys? I mean, the man can barely take his eyes off you."

"What?" Heat rushed to my cheeks. "I'm sure he's only doing his job. Carl, my boss, hired him to stick to me like glue to and from work. There was an incident on the job, and he's worried that I'm a target."

Mari gathered her long glossy hair in her hands then dropped it behind her shoulders. Both she and Liv fell silent. Liv was the first to speak. "You don't sound sure that there's a threat. Always trust your instincts, and if you can't tell, listen to Trev's."

"Look, I'm not one to rely on a man," Mari said, and Liv shook her head. The dark-haired woman shoved the other's shoulder. "Unless I'm in a dire situation and am forced to."

Liv giggled. "That's not how I heard the story told."

Mari rolled her eyes. "Not the point. You know I can take care of myself, Liv."

"Yeah, yeah…"

Mari huffed then gave Liv her back, again focusing on me. "The guys are good at what they do. Trust me. We both know what we're talking about."

I stirred the tomatoes for a few minutes before answering. "I do trust him, but I'm not sure anything is going on. A lot of the small incidents can be explained away by how spacey I am —except for the screen saver, which was weird." No one had come forward to confess, but if it was just a prank, they should have by then.

The conversation about Trev stopped, and we went back to cooking, which helped me to relax in more ways than one. Liv pulled out everything we needed for the dining room table, and she and Mari set it. It would be a big meal with all of us sitting there, especially when the two I hadn't yet met, Jack and Hannah, joined us. With how much I liked Mari and Liv, I was hoping the same would happen with Hannah, only my impression of the tall blonde was anything but comforting.

TREV

THE DOOR TO LIAM'S OFFICE clicked behind me, and I took my seat with Liam, Chris, Jack, and Hannah. I was glad they were there already—I wanted to hash it out and make a determination where Jules was concerned. Something was going on that I couldn't put my finger on.

Jack cleared his throat. "We looked into the first group of soldiers Jules gave the injections to."

If one of the military guys was behind Jules's problems at work and home, that would explain a lot. "Find anything?"

"No." Jack tapped a pen on Liam's desk. "They were all accounted for. Their alibis and whereabouts checked out. The only thing that was flagged was the wife of one of the soldiers who had to go to the ER for a broken arm."

"We're pretty sure her husband broke it," Hannah chimed in.

"It's being handled." Liam pressed a few buttons on his laptop and flipped it around so we could see the picture of the guy. "Tim Reynolds. He's been cited for anger problems above what we'd consider normal. I've alerted a guy in the military criminal-investigations unit. He won't mess around. If the guy is guilty, he'll make sure the wife is safe and Tim is held responsible for his actions."

"That's good, but we're back at square one, then. You're sure no one displayed any obsessive tendencies or popped up anywhere on the grid close to Jules's home or work?"

"So far, none have," Hannah responded to my question. "The second group hasn't yielded anything, either. So that leaves us without any leads. Could it be a coworker? Or a friend of one of the people who got the injection?"

I cleared my throat. "A coworker was my best guess, too, but her boss was sure it was one of the soldiers." I'd had my doubts, and it looked like they were right. "Then there's the outbreak in Russia they're collaborating on. I don't see how it could be anyone from there, but we should probably check to be safe."

"Definitely," Liam replied. "I'll talk with Rich and see what I can learn."

I nodded then turned to my brother. "Chris, did anything turn up from the screen-saver message?"

"It was changed directly from her computer. So we're either dealing with a colleague or…"

Shit. I don't like where this is going. The evidence was unusual, but there was no way Jules was responsible. My gaze bounced to each of their solemn faces. "What're you insinuating?"

Jack leaned forward, his elbows resting on his knees. "Look at the evidence so far. You've got the message on her computer that says 'remember me,' and then she fell overboard—and she was the only one. Then there was her purse that'd been moved in her house, and then her assistant commits suicide by carving a wound into her arm identical to Jules's scar?"

Hannah placed her hand on Jack's thigh. "We can't rule Jules out as a suspect. There's the problem of her missing background and her lack of childhood memories. Is she hiding a mental illness?"

Hell no. This is bullshit. "You met her. That's a ridiculous assumption." There were many accounts of people with dangerous mental disorders who committed horrible crimes against others, but I couldn't see Jules as being one of them. There was one way to get to the bottom of their concerns.

"It's not her." I took a deep breath to calm down. "If you want to reassure yourselves, use Hannah's skills to determine if those suspicions are grounded and need further evaluation."

She nodded. "Now's a perfect time. I'll go to the kitchen and… observe."

Jack's lips twitched. "We wouldn't expect you to actually cook, babe."

She yawned before standing. "We're done here?"

"Pretty much. You'll handle background checks for her colleagues, Chris?"

He nodded. "Look, we all like her, and we'll assume she isn't the one causing the problems, but we need to examine every avenue to rule out what doesn't add up."

I knew he was right, even though I didn't like it. I scrubbed my face with my hands, not liking the turn the meeting had taken. Hannah walked out, leaving the rest of us in the office. She was a highly trained former Russian spy. If any of us could strip through someone's cover, she could.

Despite my confidence that Jules was who she had portrayed to me, I worried about what Hannah would find.

ELEVEN

JULES

A BREEZE RUSTLED THROUGH THE trees on Liam and Liv's property. It was gorgeous there. I relaxed into a lounge chair and took a sip of coffee. In the distance, I watched the crest and roll of the waves. The sun sparkled off the ocean like jewels scattered by the gods.

I was alone on the back patio and didn't mind one bit. Liv had apologized for not keeping me company while I had coffee. There was no need, and I understood. She had a deadline for a new sculpture. She'd said we would have lunch together, and I looked forward to that. I needed time to grieve, to allow the void of Fran's loss to come to the forefront. Wiping the telltale trail of wetness from my cheeks, I welcomed the numbness as it crawled through my body.

I'd claimed the right to cook, and neither Liv nor Mari had argued but said they would help. I loved cooking, especially for a large group. It was the Italian in me and something my mom and I had enjoyed doing together. But instead of making me sad, I felt fulfilled for the first time in a long while. Trev's friends—his family—were great.

Mari stepped onto the patio, her long hair darker from a recent shower. She was exotic and gorgeous. I should have been self-conscious around the women, but Liv and Mari hadn't made me feel that way.

Hannah had, though. She'd popped into the kitchen when we were finishing up and properly introduced herself, and her eyes seemed to cut right through me. I'd felt exposed and wasn't even sure why. It was as if she was digging through my layers to see my soul. I silently wished her luck. My entire psyche ached. While the others had asked how I was doing from Fran's passing, Hannah seemed to silently judge me. I wasn't sure how I felt about that.

Mari plopped down next to me, stretching her legs out in front of her then crossing them at her ankles. "Hey, are you doing all right?"

I smiled. "I'm okay."

"I know how hard it is to lose someone you care deeply for. My aunt passed away before I met Chris. Each day out from saying goodbye gets a little easier."

"I'm finding that to be true, but her absence is so…"

"Raw?" Mari offered.

"Yes." I needed a change of subject. "It's so beautiful here."

"It is." Mari's wedding band sparkled in the sunlight. "Chris and I moved here and built a house not too long ago."

"How did you two meet?"

She chuckled, and the sound was rich and inviting. "We met in a very dangerous jungle in South America."

When the glass door slider clicked shut, we both turned to see who'd come outside. My heart kicked up a notch as Trev made his way toward us. He wore a long-sleeved gray shirt that stretched across his well-defined chest. His hand settled on my shoulder, his eyes inquisitive. I gave him a small smile. I would be okay. A few seconds passed before his inspection eased and the gravity of the moment faded.

"I've come to rescue you." He winked at me, and I managed a grin—if he only knew how true that was. "Can't have my evil sis-in-law filling your head with lies."

Mari glared at him, but I caught the amusement that crossed her expression and relaxed. She didn't seem like someone to mess with. Her temper ignited quickly, and she had a thing for knives. Twice, I'd witnessed her flipping one in her hand in a catch and release that sent alarm skating through my body.

"What do you want, ogre?"

My mouth dropped at Mari's term. *Does she not see him? He's many a woman's fantasy, including mine.*

"Evil incarnate. I'm taking Jules grocery shopping to get away from your bad influence."

Mari snorted then stood and stormed off, knocking into Trev with her shoulder. He chuckled. Behind his back, she turned and gave me a little wave. If they didn't look so different, I would have thought they were brother and sister, given how they verbally sparred.

Trev reached out and pulled me from the chair. "Liv mentioned you wanted to get a few groceries for lunch."

"I do. Thanks." We walked through the house, and I rinsed my coffee mug and put it in the dishwasher. "Let me grab my purse."

"You won't need it." He threaded his fingers through mine and tugged me toward the Jeep.

Sparks spread from my fingers, up my arm, and into my traitorous heart, which hadn't gotten the memo not to get too involved. My reaction to Trev didn't mean anything. His family was warm and comfortable with each other. He was making sure I kept up with him, and that was all. I couldn't afford to read anything into it, especially since I wasn't sure how much longer he'd be around.

He held the door open, and I climbed inside. After he got in, we pulled out onto the long driveway, leaving me to get lost in my thoughts. I wondered whether there was any need for Trev to continue to work for me. The only things that lacked an explanation were the screen saver and the message in my bathroom mirror, which I hadn't told him about because it likely had been a figment of my imagination—one of those strange memory fragments seen from an omniscient perspective. The rest, well, I was known to walk around with my head in the clouds when I was preoccupied, especially when puzzling over an issue at work.

As we approached a small town, I stopped worrying about everything and decided to enjoy the moment. Besides, I would get to cook lunch and maybe dinner, too, though if the last two days were any indication, I wouldn't be able to eat. I couldn't swallow more than one bite.

The town was nestled along the coast, making for a beautiful sight. We strolled along the sidewalk, and I peeked into an antique store and then a flower shop before we arrived at the grocery store. We walked inside, and Trev grabbed a shopping cart. "What do you want to get?"

I rattled off a few ingredients. We made short work of the list, and before I knew it, Trev was loading our groceries into the back seat. "Let's grab some coffee before we head back," he said as he closed the door.

I wasn't going to complain—I was a tad addicted to the stuff. I reached out and linked our hands together as we strolled down the sidewalk, following the rich smell of roasting coffee beans coming from the café on the harbor.

As soon as I realized what I'd done, I let go of him and asked myself what I was doing. I slanted my gaze to gauge his reaction. He didn't seem fazed at all as he opened the door and held it for me. I walked under his arm without ducking. We placed our orders, and when they were ready, we went back outside.

"It's lovely here." There was something so quaint about the area, even though it wasn't a stereotypical small town. The ruggedness of coastal Maine spoke to me, as did the miles of white-sand beaches. The area had charm in spades from lighthouses, friendly shops, the promise of lobster, and if I was up to it, boating.

"It is beautiful." He took a sip of his drink while we strolled to his Jeep. "I've thought of relocating, now that my brother and Mari don't live in California anymore. It's still a possibility, but I'm not ready yet."

I ignored the disappointment that flashed at the thought of him moving away from me. "Would you live nearer to the winery or your brother?"

Trev's arm slipped around me, and he pulled me close to him as we moved around a man walking his dog. Despite my jackhammering pulse, I did my best not to read into his actions. All the touching was nothing. He was simply making sure I was out of the way of the other people on the sidewalk. I couldn't fabricate something that wasn't there, even if each time he held me, I wanted to soften and mold myself to him. He overloaded my senses.

By the time we got back to Liv and Liam's place, my mind began to function again, and even more after we'd piled the grocery bags on the counter. The girls walked in and pushed Trev from the kitchen. Liv turned to me, rubbing her hands together. "What are we making?"

I laughed as I rattled off the names of the dishes, mushroom risotto paired with a big Italian salad and bruschetta on the side. Hannah moved forward, and I shivered. She intimidated me. I couldn't help it. She was tall and lean with platinum hair that fell past her shoulders and icy-blue eyes that bore holes into my soul, mining for my deepest, darkest thoughts. *Wow, I am dramatic.*

"I'd like to help." Hannah leaned against the counter. Outwardly, she appeared relaxed, but she reminded me of a snake, coiled and ready to strike.

Mari fell quiet beside me, and I turned to see what was wrong.

"You'll have to excuse Mari's weird behavior. It's just that… we met under difficult circumstances. That's all water under the bridge, isn't it, Mari?" Hannah's furrowed brows dared Mari to deny what she'd said.

I curbed my tongue, even though I wanted to ask what her problem was with me and what I'd done to cause suspicion.

"Why do you want to cook, Hannah? Not really your thing, now, is it?" Mari held her gaze, countering with a fierce frown of her own.

Normally I didn't care if I got a less than friendly welcome, but I sort of did that time.

"Hey, knock it off." Liv wedged herself between Mari and Hannah. She caught my gaze. "They're basically like sisters now, which means they fight as family does, only they're frightening when they do."

That I could believe. Something told me there was an underlying reason for the way Hannah was acting, which could explain why Mari had picked up on it. I wasn't sure it was something I wanted to know.

TWELVE

TREV

THICK GRAY CLOUDS ROLLED OVERHEAD as I pulled up to Jules's beach house after running out to get gas. She wasn't dealing with being back in California well and wanted a few minutes to finish getting ready. The trip to Maine had obviously helped Jules process her grief a little and provided a good distraction, until we had to leave very early that morning to get back home, where she faced an onslaught of pain. Liv and Mari were a godsend, as was Hannah. Before we left, the guys and I had convened again with her to hear her assessment. She didn't suspect Jules, and that was enough for all of us.

I paused with my hand on the car door as her front door banged shut behind her. Before I could get out, she was already running to the truck as fat drops of rain fell from the sky.

Pale and with half-moons painted beneath her eyes, she climbed into my vehicle. Her hand shook as she shoved a few thick strands of dark-brown hair from her face.

"Are you okay?" I brushed some hair off her forehead.

She said nothing, just nodded, which was another cause for concern. I didn't blame her, as we were headed to Fran's funeral. Nothing about the day would be easy or okay.

Thunder rumbled in an angry growl as I pulled away from the curb. More drops of rain splashed across the windshield, and the sky darkened. It was fitting.

Jules shivered beside me, and I cranked up the heat, even

though it was already warm in the SUV. Her chill likely came from what she would soon face—saying her final goodbye to her assistant and friend. It sucked, and with my line of work and upbringing, I understood it too well.

We pulled up to the funeral home in silence. I got out of the truck, went around to her side, then opened her door. Her hand trembled as I laced our fingers together. I didn't care how it looked to her boss. I needed to touch her. Her soft skin slid against my rough palm. I wanted to pull her close and shelter her with my body, but I had to let her do her thing, and I needed to do mine. The small touch had to be enough.

With slow steps, we walked along the sidewalk to the funeral home's entrance. After the proceedings, there would be a family-only burial. I pushed the door open, and we entered the parlor. The soft glow of table and overhead lamps lent to the quiet murmur of the people inside. There were a lot of them. We weaved through until we had a view of where Fran was laid out. The crowd increased as we neared the casket. My hand rested against Jules's lower back. She shook like a leaf, grief emanating from her in crushing waves.

The funeral home was decorated in soft, muted colors. The light cast a warm amber glow over the tan-and-wood interior. A box of tissues was on each table's surface. A mix of comfortable armchairs and a couch were in the back of the room, filled with grieving people, as was the lobby. We moved more deeply into the viewing room, weaving through a press of dark-clad colleagues and friends conversing in low murmurs. Rows of chairs faced the raised platform where Fran rested.

We took our turn at the casket, and a sob slipped from Jules's lips. I wished I could hold and comfort her, but all I could do was offer support by being there. My open palm rested on her lower back, letting her know she wasn't alone.

The casket was open, and Fran's hands were arranged one over the other, the gruesome incision effectively covered. While she stood next to Fran, I scanned the crowd. Each of the faces

I saw held the same disbelief, grief, and shock in varying degrees. The specific way Fran had died—I didn't believe it was suicide—was no coincidence. Whoever wished Jules harm would be close by, possibly in attendance.

Murmurs of conversation buzzed while muffled sobs filled the silence when words failed. We stepped aside from saying goodbye to Fran so the next people in line could have their turn. From time to time, co-workers reached out to squeeze Jules's hand or arm. Her body shook harder, her plump lower lip trembled, and she sank her teeth into it before ducking her head.

I shifted my hand to her waist and pulled her against my body after she'd stumbled one too many times. "Jules."

Pressing further into me, she turned to a tall, thin man who approached her with sadness clinging to his frowning features.

"Peter." She reached for his hands and squeezed.

My team and I had viewed all the personnel files and background checks for everyone who had access to the research facility floor Jules was on. Peter hadn't raised a single red flag. Even so, my gut tightened, but my instincts of a threat didn't flare. *Am I jealous of a lanky scientist?* His free hand came up and covered hers, and a jolt of anger slammed into me. *Shit, I am.*

Behind wire-rimmed glasses, Peter shot anxious glances my way as he conversed with Jules. I fought the urge to grin, which was not exactly appropriate, but it was difficult to withhold the predatory smile I wanted to flash. *Yeah, be nervous. She's with me.* The corner of my mouth twitched.

The guys would get a laugh out of my reaction. I'd never found anyone that made me act like, well, one of them, at least among my brother, Liam, Matt, and Jack. The rest were single, which I technically was too. *Do I want to be?* My hand tightened on Jules's waist. Even as small as she was, she fit against my side as if we'd been made for each other. I wanted to pursue whatever was growing between us.

By the fifth nervous glance from Peter, I pulled fully out of my thoughts and listened to what he was saying.

"A bunch of us are going out for drinks after… Do you want to go with?"

His hopefulness made me want to growl.

"Thanks, Peter, but I want to go home. It's been a tough week, and the next one will be…"

Hell. I knew that's what she wanted to say. The next day at work, she would feel Fran's absence excruciatingly. My gut told me that the mishaps and accidents happening around her weren't a result of her actions, as my team had worried. Instead, someone wanted to make her vulnerable. Whatever was going on, I would have to stay vigilant to make sure no one got to her.

JULES

RAIN BEADED AGAINST THE CAR window and left trails as it slid down the pane. The wind howled, and the clouds rolled, threatening to unleash a torrential downpour at any moment. It was fitting. I wanted to curl into a ball and cry for Fran. I never knew she was depressed. They said she'd slit her wrist and taken her life, but it didn't make sense at all. More often than not, she was happy or yelling to counter my quick temper. We were friends and colleagues, and I had no idea what I was going to do without her.

Trev pulled up the driveway to my home, and shock jolted down my body, leaving tingles in its wake. The front door was open. "I closed that." I turned and implored him to agree, my eyes wide as they could go. "You heard the slam."

A brief nod was all he gave me, but it was enough.

"Lock the doors behind me. Wait here." Trev left the truck

running before getting out and jogging to the yawning doorway.

No freaking way. I'm not waiting here. I felt like a sitting duck. I shut the engine off and slipped out and into the rain as quietly as I could. Not far behind Trev, I sloshed onto the soaked rug in the entryway. *Crap.* I would need to take care of that.

My heart thudded against my rib cage just as Trev reappeared before me. Frustration was evident in his tense shoulders and the grooves bracketing his mouth, which was pressed into a thin line. I knew I'd caused some of his reaction by not staying in the SUV. "The house is clear. No one is inside."

I sagged against the doorframe. He pulled me to him and shut the door behind me. "Why don't you look around to make sure nothing is missing while I take care of cleaning up the entryway."

I nodded, slipped my wet shoes off, and moved farther inside. I didn't have much of value except some earrings that had been my mom's, a broken bracelet—a replica of one given to my sister—pictures, and my mom's cookbook. In front of the bookcase that held my mom's recipes, I carefully lifted the thick binder from its shelf. It was packed full of handwritten notes and coveted recipes, and relief washed over me that it was still there. I didn't know why I thought it wouldn't be—*who would steal a cookbook?*

To me, the book was invaluable. Each handwritten recipe and note was from my mom, and I couldn't ever replace them or the time spent with her that the binder symbolized. Flipping through the recipes, I stopped at the section where she'd tucked a letter in between the pages for me. A few more tears ran down my cheeks, following the same tracks that'd been left behind from Fran's funeral. *I miss you, Mom.* My fingers traced her flowing script. *Juliana*—no one called me by my full name except her. I missed hearing her say it with her Italian lilt.

While the things that'd been happening to or around me were odd and heartbreaking, I didn't think the instances warranted opening Pandora's letter. I knew I couldn't open it just because I missed her and wanted to read what she'd written to feel closer to her.

I closed the binder then put it safely back on its shelf. With every step through each room, I had the sense that someone had been in my house. The energy felt different.

I figured I was probably making myself crazy and hurried back to where Trev was mopping up the excess water just inside the front door.

"It's windy. Could be that the door didn't latch when you left. You ran out in a rush. Maybe you forgot to lock it. Either way, I'll review the security footage."

I shrugged, still looking around to see if anything was out of place. "Maybe." Then I saw it: the small side table by the front door had held a small picture of Mom, but it wasn't there. Frantically, I turned, trying to find it.

On the coffee table in the living room, the frame was angled perfectly to face whoever sat on the couch.

Someone *had* been there.

THIRTEEN

I BREEZED THROUGH SECURITY AT the front entry, barely acknowledging the guard on duty, swiped my ID, rode the elevator, and entered the lab. It was Monday, and it felt like one. The travel mug of coffee was my life force. I'd had two cups, and I would need another one after I finished what I had. It was going to be that kind of day or week.

"Jules." Carl popped his head in before I made it to my desk.

"Yes. Just let me put my purse away." *But not the coffee. That's going with me.* I rounded a few tables until I arrived at my station and jerked to a stop. *Shit.* A collection tray of test tubes sat on my desk. My eyes narrowed then went wide. They were mine. *I couldn't have done that, could I have?*

I dropped my purse in a drawer and felt the tubes. They were cool to the touch. I didn't understand. The last time I'd been in the lab was on Friday. We never left our work out. *What is going on?*

I sagged against the side of the desk. *I'm going crazy. Seriously, I can't handle this.* Taking the chance of making Carl mad by not heading to his office right away, I grabbed my cell and pressed the right contact number to connect to Trev. I'd shown him the picture of Mom the night before and where the frame used to sit. The door being open and the moved photo added up to seem like more than my usual scatterbrained ways. And I didn't leave the collection tray out. I couldn't have. If I had, the tubes would have been room temperature, the experiment that held one of the Russian's biopsies compromised. It wouldn't have stayed cold for two days. Someone had done it deliberately, and that time, I knew it hadn't been me.

Trev answered right away. "You okay?"

"Yeah, I think so. But—"

"What's wrong?" His voice cracked like a whip through the speaker.

Shit. I'm being paranoid. "One of my experiments was left out on my desk this morning. It's still cool, like it hasn't been out of the refrigerated storage long."

"Is anyone else there?"

"No. I mean, yes. Carl is, and a few others are." *God, I'm an idiot.* "I shouldn't have called. I bet it was Carl." I glanced around the open room that held a few desks, tables with equipment lining one side of the room, and storage along the back. No one else who'd worked on the project seemed to be in yet.

"You did the right thing, Jules. If you're scared or think something's wrong, I want you to get ahold of me immediately. It probably was Carl, but you should ask to make sure. Do you want me to come? I can hang out there today."

"Ah, no."

Trev laughed. "It's not a problem. You won't even know I'm there."

I couldn't help it—I snorted. "Are you aware of the riot you'll cause with the female population within this office?" *With Sandy?* "No work will get done."

"You're exaggerating."

I could hear the smile in his voice, and my shoulders relaxed. He made things better. I grinned as if he could see me. "Thanks, Trev. It helped to talk it through with you." I shook my head as we said goodbye, wondering when he had wormed his way into my heart. There was no denying it anymore: I cared about him.

I dropped my cell into my lab-coat pocket, and with one

more glance at the test tubes on my desk, I went in search of Carl.

I tapped lightly on his doorframe, and Carl lifted his head from whatever papers he was reviewing.

"You wanted to see me?"

"Yes." He motioned for me to come in, and a deep sigh filled the air. "Fran will be missed. How are you holding up?"

Not great. I miss her. And at work, I felt her absence the most. "Putting one foot in front of the other. Some moments are okay. Others are more difficult."

I sank into one of the plush seats he had in front of his desk. I'd always wondered why he had such comfortable chairs for others to sit on. I would have thought he would want us in and out as quickly as possible.

He dropped the pen he'd been holding and leaned back, giving me his full attention.

Before we started with whatever he wanted to talk about, I needed answers. "Do you know anything about the new trials that were left on my desk this morning? I put everything away before the weekend, and the vials were cool to the touch so…"

Carl's brows furrowed. "No, I can't say that I do. But it could have been your new lab assistant pulling it out, trying to anticipate what you'd need first thing. Which is what I wanted to talk to you about. Peter has been assigned to help you, at least for a few weeks."

I opened my mouth to protest, but he held up his hand, his palm facing me.

"Just for a few weeks, Jules. If he doesn't fit, I'll find you someone who will, but you need help."

I scowled at him. "I'm capable of doing the work without someone fetching everything I need."

Carl chuckled. *Damn him.*

"I know you can, but when you're chasing a cure, on the verge of discovery, you lose track of time."

It was true. During those situations, I'd lost track of hours, skipped lunch and dinner, and fallen asleep at my desk only to wake up at work the next morning. A few times, I'd fumbled vital experiments due to my preoccupation with solving a work-related problem. I crossed my arms, exhausted and not wanting to admit he was right. "Fine. I'll try to cooperate with Pete as my assistant."

Carl shuffled the papers on his desk. "That's all I ask."

I shifted in my seat, mulling over a problem that I couldn't let go. "Do special teams like Trev's have access to the restricted military vector if they go to one of the high-risk territories?"

"No." He drummed his fingers on his desk. "If Trev's private military team is called in, there is very little preparation time. They aren't government employees any longer, and they don't have access to all the shots, especially ones like what you've developed."

"I want them to. I want a batch specifically on hand, should they deploy to any of the hot spots. Or I could administer the tool kit to them within the month."

He shook his head.

I crossed my arms over my chest. "This is important to me."

His eyes took on a speculative gleam as he drummed his fingers on the desk. "I'll see what I can do. In the meantime, how is the wound salve progressing?"

"Well. I'm almost there." My thumb slipped beneath the cuff of my lab coat and traced over the old scars. The salve was close to my heart and very near completion. "I have some more testing to do, and then I'll have a better time line for you." I tugged at a loose string on my coat. "Did Dr. Mikhailov receive the antibody vials?"

"He did, and they've helped tremendously. I'll forward his response and the developments he's reported since the injections were given."

"Thanks. I'm glad we could help." I wanted to ask about

the tool-kit leak, but maybe not just then. Carl would handle that and figure out who was responsible.

"Then get back to work." He winked, which took any sting from his words.

I grinned. He would push until he got what he wanted, but I didn't mind. Science was my drug. I was obsessive about my experiments, and if it wasn't for needing to sleep, I would probably have worked until I dropped. Fran used to have to drag me away. With that thought, my shoulder slammed into the hallway wall.

My feet dragged as I neared my desk, where Peter greeted me with a smile. My gut churned. I didn't understand why he seemed to be so happy, nor was I pleased that we would be sharing a workspace.

"I want to let you know I'm grateful for the opportunity to work with you."

"Thanks, Peter." I wanted to take a step back from his enthusiasm. I found it odd that we were paired in the first place, as he hadn't worked as an assistant before, so I wondered why he had been assigned to me. That seemed below his skill level.

"Fran was very lucky to be included in your research for the tool kit." Behind his wire-rimmed glasses, his eyes sparkled with excitement. "Do you have ideas for another tool kit?"

Oh, that's his angle? To be linked with me in case I make another discovery? I got the impression his career hadn't been going as he'd hoped—no scientist who already had a secure position would take one that was beneath them. "Nothing new right now. We need to tie up everything with the three projects I've been working on." It was busy work that he'd unknowingly signed up for in order to work for me. It was going to be a very long day. I wondered how long he would last.

FOURTEEN

SWEAT DRIPPED FROM MY CHIN, tickling as it rolled into my sports bra. I needed to run. Yesterday, working with Peter had been trying, and I expected a similar experience today. I lengthened my stride, my running shoes pounding against the shoreline beside Trev's. He increased his speed, and I did the same. Even though he had longer legs, I kept up with him, at least for the most part. I was determined to beat him. Losing in Maine and cooking breakfast hadn't been a big deal, but I wanted to win.

Loose sand chased us every step of the way, but I was rarely a klutz while running. With each swing of my arms, the wind and endorphins lessened the grief over losing Fran. It wasn't gone, just manageable.

Music pumped through my earbuds, and I let the rhythm fuel me. Salty sea spray kissed my right side as a gust of wind hurled the droplets our way. I tucked my chin, lengthened my stride, and flew.

The thudding of his feet and the idea of him catching me spurred me to push harder in anticipation of winning. Like always, my mind eased into a runner's high. The race became about the beach, my inner thoughts free to drift. Calculations danced through my head. While my body worked, my anxiety lessened, allowing another level of thinking that I craved.

Running gave me the freedom to work on problems, either work or personal, and find plausible solutions. When the chemical makeup of the healing salve I'd been stuck on came to the forefront of my thoughts, I pulled apart the issues, isolated them, and toyed with answers. As my foot crossed the imaginary finish line we'd set, I saw clearly how to fix it.

A sense of elation flooded me as I slowed my stride and cooled down. With a glance over my shoulder, I grinned at Trev, pulled an earbud out, and blew him a kiss. "I won."

He'd decreased his pace, too, until I'd taunted him. Mischief danced in his eyes, and my heart skipped a beat. In two strides, he was on me. I squealed as his sweaty arms wrapped around my waist. When he pivoted toward the water, I turned into an octopus. I wound my legs and arms tightly around him. "If you even think about it…"

Deep laughter teased my ear, and I shivered as his lips grazed the sensitive lobe. I jerked against him, my legs tightening even more. *What was that?*

We'd stopped inches from the shoreline, and I couldn't help but notice how he felt against me. I was clinging to his chest, every delicious curve and dip of hard muscle pressed against me. I wanted him. Fighting my attraction to him was more energy than it was worth, and him holding me like that made me think he was attracted to me too.

He tugged on my ponytail, and I eased my grip on his neck enough that we could look at each other. I caught my lower lip with my teeth. His eyes were dilated, intense. *Will he kiss me? Should I kiss him?*

The breeze picked up, and I shivered. He closed the distance, and my eyes drifted closed. At the first brush of his lips over mine, I threaded my fingers through his hair. His tongue traced my bottom lip before he deepened the kiss. Heat spread through me with each caress, chasing the chill away.

When he pulled back, I lifted heavy eyelids to his burning gaze. Unwinding my legs, I dangled until he lowered me to the sand. His arm around my waist kept me steady. I wanted more.

His thumb caressed my cheek, and then he smiled. "That was nice."

I shivered again as his deep voice sent aftershocks along my sensitive skin. "Yes." I almost groaned aloud. *That's all I can say? Yes?* Kissing him was like a sedative to my racing mind.

His hand trailed down my arm until he threaded his fingers through mine. We turned as one and began to walk back toward my house. I wanted more. "Is this going to complicate things between us?"

He snorted. "Were they ever not complicated?"

"True." I worried my lower lip. He had a point. The tension between us had been high for a while, but I'd assumed it was mostly one-sided. "Was this a one-time thing?"

"I don't want it to be. Do you have any issues seeing where this might go while I'm working as your bodyguard?"

"I'm not the one who hired you." With a shake of my head, I grinned. "I don't have any problem with us. Oh, that reminds me—"

"What does? That I guard your body?" Mischief danced in his eyes, and he flashed that panty-melting grin.

I understood why the other female scientists acted silly around him. At that point, I was too. "No, not that. Work. I was thinking about how the military has access to the vaccines my team created."

"Ah, the miracle shot your boss raved over? I was under the impression you were the mastermind behind that one."

Heat flooded my cheeks. Carl needed to stop telling Trev things about me. "I did, but it was a team effort to bring it to production." I waved away his laughter. "Anyway, the military has access to it, but not private contractors like you and your partners."

"We used to when we were active-duty Navy SEALs. Now that we're sort of out—"

"Once a SEAL always a SEAL." Even I knew that phrase.

"Exactly. But out of direct active duty, we don't get the latest and greatest meds any longer."

"I disagree with that practice. Your team does search and rescue in dangerous countries. Carl agreed that I could administer the gene-mutation injection to you all, should you want it."

His eyebrows furrowed. "What exactly does the shot do, and are there side effects?"

Excitement ping-ponged along my nervous system. I loved what I did and could talk to him about it for hours. "The tool kit I developed targets the CCR5 gene, a protein receptor that sits on the outside of white blood cells. The genetically engineered injection precisely targets and edits DNA. The result is a mutation process to become CCR5-delta 32. The mutation grants immunity to harmful diseases such as HIV or lethal hemorrhagic fevers." Trev's expression glazed over, and I fought a smile. *Should I have explained it another way?*

"I'm not exactly following."

"Do you remember about a year ago when the US embassy overseas had a sudden mice and rat infestation?"

"Yes." His gaze sharpened. "Several employees and soldiers lost their lives."

"Hemorrhagic fevers use the CCR5 as an entry point to gain access to the immune system. If they had the genetically engineered procedure done or naturally carried the mutation, their bodies would not have contracted the disease."

"What does the tool kit do? I mean, how does it alter someone's genes?"

"It's not a definite that a recipient's chromosomes will be altered by the tool kit and vector. But there is a high chance during the incubation procedure that they will. Think of a strand of marbles. Their surface is smooth, glassy."

"Okay."

"Then think of a pitted or spiky rubber ball. If both those

objects roll through loose debris, what we'll call the disease, which will pick up traces of it?"

"The spiky one. Okay, I understand the difference caused by the mutation, but the process is mind-blowing."

"I get that. Several years ago, this process was stumbled upon, more or less. Genes have been edited to resist diseases in a few scenarios. There was a lot of controversy about how ethical the practice was. Some of the cases reported were done on human embryos. That's not what this vector is for. It's for consenting adults only."

"I heard something about that. A doctor tampered with an embryo."

"Yes, he performed gene editing before a baby—twins, actually—were born. That's not how this formula is to be used.

"There is another case of a man who went through many rounds of chemotherapy. When his immune system was severely compromised, he was given large doses of antibodies that contained delta-32. He survived, and his DNA then carried the mutation."

"With this injection, do we have to go through chemo?" Trev frowned.

"No. It's a targeted injection. It's not the most comfortable procedure, but there won't be any chemo involved."

He nodded. "Good. I wasn't even a little on board if there was."

I laughed. "You're good. But there are a lot of factors into bringing about the chromosomal mutation, and it doesn't work for everyone. We have had some resistant cases. And since it's a relatively new procedure, we aren't positive of long-term effects for the next generations. Although if we look at history in Europe, the mutation naturally occurred in about one in every ten thousand. Over time, that number increased to one in ten.

"The science behind the injection is sound. The technique utilized is called CRISPR." I loved talking about that stuff—it settled any nerves I had. It was my thing. "I have every faith that there will not be issues due to the forced genetic alterations. Faced with what our soldiers have been attacked with, the risk of the procedure seems worth it. Of course, the choice is yours and your team's. I could go into a lot of detail if you need me to about the injection and what happens when it's introduced into the bloodstream."

My gaze lingered on his lips. He listened, making me feel important even though he had to be bored to tears while I essentially geeked out—*I want to kiss him.* I shook my head and dove back into my long explanation for my current work.

"That's not necessary right now. I'm impressed." He squeezed my hand. "Would you mind sharing the details over a call with my team? I'm not sure I'll be able to repeat everything the same as you said, and I'm sure they will have questions."

"Of course." I couldn't help it—my mind wandered again to the kiss we'd shared. I had a feeling that our relationship was going to become even more complicated.

FIFTEEN

JULES

THE NEXT DAY DAWNED BRIGHTLY, and the sun pierced through wispy white clouds and bounced off several reflective pairs of sunglasses worn by the people walking in the opposite direction. My stomach growled again, and I glanced to the right to gauge how far I was from the sandwich shop. Becs chatted in my earpiece, and I waited for her to take a breath so that I could share my news. We'd planned to catch up during our lunch breaks that day. I wished she was closer, but chatting on the phone was the next best thing.

Suddenly, the toe of my flat caught on a raised sidewalk edge. *Shit.* My arms went out to brace my fall as I stumbled. A hand shot out and steadied me, the grip so tight on my elbow that I knew it would bruise. As quickly as I'd been grabbed, the person released me. I took a non-stumbling step forward then looked to my left to thank whoever had saved me from a very unfortunate face-plant.

Pedestrian traffic flowed at a fast clip while I scanned the faces. Not one person caught my gaze or gave any indication that they'd helped me, which I found odd. After a glance behind and to the right, I gave up. Good thing, too, because Becs's tirade about her coworker had finally ended.

"Okay, that sucks. I hope she gets demoted." There was nothing worse than a colleague trying to claim your work as their own. "But I've got to tell you this before I burst."

"What?" Dread coated Becs's voice, not that I blamed her.

My life had been a series of horrible events, from the company breach of my screen saver to Fran's death.

What I was about to share was different. "Trev kissed me."

"The hot bodyguard? The same guy you went away with for a weekend and *nothing* happened? That one?"

"Hilarious. But yes, same guy."

Becs squealed. "It's about damn time!"

"It's weird? I mean, I shouldn't cross that line, at least not while he's contracted with Carl to watch over me."

"And how exactly is he watching over you?'

I stifled a giggle. "Stop. It's not like that. It was just a kiss."

"Are you saying all this with him beside you?" Becs's voice rose an octave.

"No," I snickered. "I didn't tell him I was going out to lunch. He committed to teaching women's self-defense classes this afternoon. That's important, and honestly, it's lunchtime. It's super busy. Nothing should happen with all these people around."

"Be careful, Jules. I worry about you."

"I am."

At the sandwich shop, I pushed open the door and got in line at the register. I'd already phoned in my order, so I didn't need to wait behind all the other customers to eat lunch, which was much easier, especially given that my break was short.

Becs chatted away, amusing herself as usual.

"You're crazy," I said, rolling my eyes at her shenanigans. It was a single kiss—an exceptional one, but not a declaration of love. I found a seat and munched on my loaded pastrami sandwich while she gossiped about the new scientist, whom she'd nicknamed Clark Kent.

"You know that's the wrong reference, right? Clark Kent was a reporter, not a scientist. You'd be closer calling him Peter Parker."

"Also a reporter, I think." Becs loudly munched on chips as she defended her name choice. "Steve fits the label. You haven't seen him. Remember the new *Superman* movie, the one with Henry Cavill?"

"Oh, dark hair, blue eyes? Super hot?"

"Ding-ding-ding! That's what this guy looks like, but Steve doesn't have heterochromia. That small patch of brown on Henry's left eye makes him unique and sexy as hell. I figured Clark Kent was better than what I wanted to call him, which was Hotness or Beefcake."

I choked on the sip of water I'd just taken. Coughing, I wiped tears from my eyes. Thank God the little café was packed and loud. Few people paid attention to me. "You're certifiable, Becs."

"Maybe, but it takes one to know one."

"You're not wrong there." I popped the last bite of my sandwich into my mouth. "I've got to get back to work. Love ya."

We hung up, and I tossed my sandwich wrapper and headed out the door. Weaving through people on the busy sidewalk, I moved close to the buildings to avoid being jostled. Phone in hand, I thumbed through a few emails checking for urgent messages, careful not to run into anyone.

A hard tug on my shirt threw me off-balance. I glanced up, disoriented as I was lifted off my feet, opening my mouth to yell. A hand clamped over my lips. The scream stalled in my throat as a man dragged me back into darkened walkway between two buildings. My back was plastered against his chest. I struggled, and my heart kicked into overdrive. I had to break his hold.

We went deeper into the alleyway, away from people. *No.* Thinking about what could happen could have frozen me, but I kicked back. The grunt behind me provided only a short-lived sense of satisfaction. So I squirmed then went limp. Anything to escape.

"Stop," the man growled.

No freaking way. I delivered another solid kick. If I could only angle a little higher, I could catch him where it counted. I wheezed. The arm banded around my waist shifted to my ribs and tightened. I couldn't inflate my lungs to take a full breath. Tears gathered in my eyes, and another wave of panic crested.

"Calm down," his deep, hoarse voice hissed in my ear.

Oh my God, he's going to kill me repeated over and over in my oxygen-starved brain. In slow increments, the crushing hold loosened enough for me to take a full breath. My lungs filled painfully. Seconds passed, and I gulped air through my nose like a drug.

"We have an understanding now?"

My body shook, my back still pinned against his chest. Even though I couldn't see him, I knew it was the same guy as the one who'd pushed me. The stale smell of smoke clung to his hand and clothes. I got out a muffled "yes" as I continued to evaluate and categorize anything and everything around me, on the off chance he would release me or I could escape.

His hand left my mouth but trailed down to my neck, where he wrapped my throat in a firm but not too restricting grip. Black hair covered his deeply tanned arm—not too much, but enough for me to know he wasn't a blond. I couldn't detect much else. The smell of cigarettes overpowered everything else.

"You've taken something from me. Now you owe me." His thumb caressed my skin while his palm remained firmly against my throat. "I want the vector. Keep some on you at all times. If you don't have it next time, you won't like what happens."

He isn't going to kill me. Hope sparked to life. I knew I would have bruises, but it sounded like he was going to let me go. "Okay. When?" My voice shook, and I inwardly cringed knowing he could hear how frightened I was.

"I don't think so. I'll surprise you. It's not for you to know when, but make sure you have the military vector on you at all times."

Does he have an accent? I'm going with yes, though it's so faded that it only came out once. I couldn't place it. "How do you know about that?"

"It's not a closely guarded secret, sweetheart." He pressed his face to the top of my head and inhaled.

My fear spiked again, and dots swam before my eyes. "Where do you want me to meet you?"

A throaty laugh stirred the hair at the top of my head, and I smelled a hint of peppermint on his breath. *Gum? A mint?*

"I'll find you." His hand left my throat and drifted down, pausing at the top of my shirt. Two fingers dipped beneath the collar. "Remember, if I can't get to you or if you don't have it on you, you won't like the consequences."

Tremors wracked my body, and I shook in his hold. He released me enough so that my feet touched the ground once more, and I worked to ignore the hard press of either a gun or his erection at the base of my spine. Bile inched up my throat, and my mouth flooded with saliva. I swallowed convulsively. *I will not throw up.* I continued to gulp.

With a violent shove, I fell to my hands and knees. Terror held me captive. The scuffle of shoes echoed off the brick until they faded. Then there were no more. Tears splashed on the rough pavement between my hands. Gathering courage, I pushed off the ground and turned. No one was there. I was alone. A sob tore from my throat, and I walked on shaky legs to where I'd dropped my cell near the entrance of the alley.

With the tips of my fingers, I picked it up and slipped it into my pocket. The knowledge that I wasn't safe, even in public, shot through my body. I broke into a run. My office was only a block away. I could make it.

My ribs screamed as they inflated with my labored breathing. Full-on sprinting, I burst through the glass doors. Rather than heading through security, I slammed to a stop. Gasping for breath, I slumped against the front desk. Josh, the day security guard, lurched to his feet.

"What's wrong?" Hand on his gun, Josh alternated from my face to the front doors.

"Someone grabbed me." I couldn't stop the tears. "He pulled me into an alley." Embarrassed, I swiped them away as they fell.

"Are you hurt?" Josh hurried around the counter until he had my shoulders in a gentle grip."

I shook my head. "He's gone but"—God, I felt like a fool —"can you…" *What do I want, for him to walk me upstairs? That's stupid.* "Never mind. I—will you make sure no one gets through who doesn't work here?" I meant outsiders coming in for meetings.

He spoke into a handheld device, ordering security to sweep the area outside the building for anyone suspicious. "Of course, Dr. Moretti." He ushered me through the metal detector, keying me in by hand. Thank God, because there was no way my shaking hand could have pulled my keycard from my purse.

Another guard rounded the corner and took Josh's spot at the desk. Concern was etched in his kind eyes. He guided me to the elevator, pressed the button, then accompanied me inside. I worked on slowing my breathing as he questioned me about what transpired. I relayed everything I could remember, and he informed me that he would call the police so they could talk to me and file a report. I didn't want to, but it wouldn't be smart not to document what had happened.

After Josh settled me into a chair in Carl's office, he talked in hushed tones with my boss before he left. Josh had tried to help, but it wouldn't be enough for Carl. I mentally prepared to have to relay the story three more times—to him, the police, and finally Trev.

The day dragged. I wanted it to be over, but there was work to be done, and it was a safe environment, so I would stay. I took some time to settle my nerves then got back to work. Trev would pick me up in two hours. I refused to go home earlier than that, especially when I wanted to play around with the solution for the healing salve that had come to me while running with him the day before.

No new information had come from Dr. Mikhailov. They had caught the few who had been infected early, and the antibodies shot seemed to slow the progression of the fever enough to give their immune systems a fighting chance.

Time passed quickly, and before I knew it, Trev entered my workstation. He'd hung around after I spoke with the police, but I banned him from my office until it was time to go home. I needed to concentrate, and there was none of that when he was around.

Thankfully, he'd brushed off Sandy's annoying flirtation. She spent the next hour hurling daggers at me with her eyes. I couldn't help it—her jealousy and his rebuttal to her advances gave me warm fuzzies, which helped to keep me from dwelling on the attack.

I put the samples away and straightened up my workspace before I caught the stern set to his mouth. I sighed. My life was about to get very complicated.

I unlocked the cabinet that held the sought-after vector for the CRISPR, hovering over one of the vials and debating whether I should comply with my attacker's demands or fill a vial with saline. I glanced over my shoulder at Trev. The attacker wouldn't know if what I had was the right version, and there was little chance of him reaching me since Trev heard what had happened. "I don't want to give him the vector."

"You shouldn't. And while I don't think he will have an opportunity to get near you, there is always a small window. I don't want you to give him a reason to hurt you."

Or kill me. I shuddered. "Then maybe an old version of the formula. It didn't pass the tests, but he'd never know."

"I can live with that."

I shut down my monitor and rounded my desk. Trev's hand settled on the small of my back, and we made our way to the elevators. With him, I let go of all worrying. He made me feel protected.

As soon as the metal door closed, he turned to me. "You've just gained a roommate."

I figured. "You're lucky I have a spare bedroom."

"Hmm."

I snorted. "You wanted the couch instead?" I wasn't comfortable with him in my bed. Not yet. Once we crossed that line, I knew I would be a goner. My heart was already way too fond of him.

He chuckled, his hand finding the small of my back again as we stepped off the elevator on the ground floor. I waved goodbye to Josh as we passed through security. Trev ushered me to his car and shielded my body as I got in. I caught the movement of his eyes as he searched for threats while he rounded to the passenger seat then got in. The doors locked immediately.

Silence stretched between us as he pulled into traffic. I clasped my hands and cast about for something to say. I didn't want to go over what'd happened again. We'd already come up with a hypothesis that the man who'd grabbed me was probably associated with someone who'd gone through the trials for the injections, a man who wanted the vector for someone outside of the focus group. There was no other plausible way he could have known about the restricted military procedure. The worst-case scenario was that he was a terrorist acquiring the meds so they could develop an attack with deadly diseases against Americans.

Truthfully, we didn't have enough to make a firm guess about motive—at least no one had shared any other scenarios with me yet, but the search was pretty narrow. The only other possibility could be a man who had access to confidential information through either the military or our company. Neither guess sat well with me, nor did the possibility that my attacker had found out about the vector from the same leak that the

Russians had. I couldn't help but wonder if we were facing a biowarfare threat.

I'd been over every moment I could remember. Trev had grilled me thoroughly and was able to extract details I didn't realize I'd noticed, like how tall the man was. When I finally had enough, he was satisfied with my responses, at least for the time being. He'd conferred with his team, and I was confident they would figure out the puzzle of who the guy was.

Trev cleared his throat, and I jolted.

"You okay?" The concern in his voice warmed my chilled body by a few degrees.

"Yes, you startled me. I was lost in thought."

"Sorry about that. Do you want to take a walk on the beach, maybe grab food at that restaurant just off the boardwalk to take your mind off what happened today?"

"Oh." I shifted so my back angled toward the passenger window and I could look at him while he drove. "I appreciate the thought, but I don't want to be around people tonight."

A smile hovered at the corners of his mouth. "How about we take my boat out and eat dinner under the stars? It's a clear night, and the water's calm."

"Would we go far from shore?" I toyed with the strap on my purse.

"No. Just past the sandbar."

"Okay. That sounds nice." I thought about what I had in the fridge. "I can put together some pasta and bread with oil and parmesan."

"Now you're talking."

He pulled into my driveway. After he cleared the house and was sure no one was inside, I went into my room with the idea of a quick shower and a change of clothes while he waited for me in the living room. It would be dark in an hour, which gave me enough time to get cleaned up then pack dinner.

The pasta and sauce took no time at all since I had some already made in the fridge. Soon, the fragrance of the tomatoes and basil filled the kitchen, and I scooped the pasta al pomodoro into containers. I made a mental note to make it again with meat.

Trev and I left the house and drove to the dock then parked. Before I knew it, we were on the boat. Dressed in yoga pants and a long-sleeved T-shirt paired with a light jacket for the chilly fall weather, I got comfortable on the seat adjacent to his as he guided the vessel to where we would anchor for the next few hours. He was right—it was a beautiful night, and I relaxed in the comfortable chair.

Once he dropped the anchor, silence blanketed us, except for the gentle lapping of the water against the boat. I unzipped the thermal bag and took out the food containers and bottled water. We settled on the rear bench seat to eat.

Trev pulled off the lid to his and groaned. "I don't think I've ever smelled anything that good."

The way to a man's heart was supposedly through his stomach. Thanks to my mom, I could cook. I grinned. "Hope you like it." He would. The combination of fresh tomatoes and basil was amazing. I would sell my soul for food like that if I didn't know how to make it.

Stars twinkled above us, and the small amount of light from the little battery-operated lantern he'd set out bathed his handsome face in a soft glow. Butterflies took flight in my stomach when he moaned after his first bite.

"Marry me," he said.

I laughed. "You're crazy."

"And you're cooking is crazy good." He shoveled a huge bite into his mouth.

We spent hours hanging out on the boat under the stars talking. That night I would sleep well, especially with Trev in the next room.

For the first time in a long while, save for the couple of days in Maine, I took pleasure in feeding someone other than myself. I only wished my mom could have met him. She would have demanded that he eat with us every night, and the marriage proposal… Even in jest, she would have taken it to heart and had us married off. I can't say I would have fought her efforts. My heart flipped at the thought—a thought that could vanish in a moment if that man ever got his hands on me again.

SIXTEEN

JULES

SADNESS SWAM THROUGH ME AS I typed in the final results for the delta-32 test against the advanced-stage virus that mimicked an ancient, encountered version of Malburg hemorrhagic fever, research I'd started with Fran but that we didn't get to finish together. While the antibody doses would slow the RNA virus enough so each person's immune system could stand a fighting chance, the delta-32 injections proved ineffective past the first five days after exposure.

The night with Trev on his boat had been nice. I only wished that same vibe had carried through to the work day, but I couldn't help but miss my friend and assistant.

I put away the last samples and cleaned up as Sandy tapped on the door to the empty lab I was working in. She was an innately nosy colleague. I shouldn't have felt as annoyed as I did, but her mere presence always grated on my nerves. I waved her in then took off the hood of the biohazard suit I was wearing. With everything safely stored away, there wasn't any chance of infection.

Sandy entered in a flurry of bouncing curls. Her hand whipped up. In between her fingers was a bright-yellow envelope. "I saw this in the stack delivered from the mailroom. It looks personal, so I thought you'd want it right away."

After I took it from her, she leaned against the table. With my eyebrows raised, I waited for her to go. She didn't. Clearly, she wanted to see what was inside, which I figured was the real reason behind her hand delivery, as we were not friends.

Whatever. I was too tired to fight her and curious who the mail was from, hand addressed but without the sender's information. Tearing the envelope open, I withdrew a colorful greeting card with a picture of balloons and confetti on the cover. *Weird.*

"What's it say?" Sandy leaned forward.

I opened it up. A pop-up sprung from the interior, followed by a plume of powder. *Shit.* Instinctively, I held my breath, closed my eyes, and dropped the card to the table. I took several steps backward before letting myself peek from beneath my lashes.

Sandy hadn't moved. She waved a hand through the air, coughing.

"Sandy!" With frantic waves of my hand, I urged her to come toward me.

As she rushed my way, I raced to the back of the lab to start the decontamination process. We both needed a chemical wash, just in case. The ventilators would take off anything harmful in the air, but Sandy had inhaled it directly. Some coated our skin. I shoved her into the emergency shower. As she began to wash, I depressed the call button for Carl before I remembered he wasn't in.

"Peter!"

He answered immediately.

"Possible hazardous airborne chemical in lab three. Test it. Don't touch the card!" It would have to be tested for prints. "Sandy is in the decontamination shower. I'm going in next."

"On it." He disconnected.

Sandy exited out the back, then I went in. I was fairly certain my lungs were okay, but some had gotten on my face. I washed thoroughly as my mind spun. We had scrubs tucked into a sealed locker in the back. After the shower, I slipped those on, properly stowing the clothes I'd had on before.

"What was that?" Sandy screeched, her eyes wide.

"I don't know. Peter's testing it." But I did know something, and there was no way the substance wasn't harmful. "How are you feeling?"

"How do you think I'm feeling?" She went into a mild coughing fit.

"Are you nauseous? Do you feel any abdominal pain? Is anything coming up when you cough?" I had to know if she was experiencing any symptoms.

"It got in my lungs. I don't know how I feel. Nothing but the cough, I think."

I had a pretty good guess of what it was, and from the expression on her face, she did as well. "We'll know what it is soon."

We waited in silence, away from the others and in an unoccupied room to be safe. After a few more minutes, Peter entered with two IV units in tow, his face grim.

"It's anthrax mixed with baby powder."

He motioned for me to raise my sleeve, but I waved him away. "Sandy needs to go first. She inhaled it."

Peter nodded then adjusted the dosage to a higher one by hanging an additional bag. She would need more to combat the spores from germinating and killing her. George, another colleague, entered and took over inserting my IV.

After Sandy was getting a steady stream of Ciprofloxacin, she turned to me, a mix of fear and outrage pulling her features tight. "Why would anyone send you a card booby-trapped with anthrax?"

"I don't know." I didn't, at least not definitively, but I had a pretty good guess—just no name. After a deep breath in, I struggled for patience in a high-stress situation. I didn't wish her ill, but it was difficult to dredge up sympathy, as she was the one who had insisted that I open it. And I couldn't help but wonder why was she getting my mail in the first place. "Did anyone hand you that card?"

"No. I was sorting through the mail and happened to see it."

"So it was on my desk?" I wasn't following. The mailroom left our mail with Rosalie, Carl's executive assistant, who distributed it to our desks.

I shot off a text to Trev, telling him what had happened and that I was okay. He would come anyway, I knew, and I wanted him there. The police would have questions too. Sandy coughed, and I focused on her, waiting for an answer.

"I was in with Rosalie when the mail was dropped off. The card was on the top of the stack, so I told her I'd give it to you."

"Thanks." I leaned back in my chair, stuck there until the IV bag was empty. The postmark was from our city. That man who'd threatened me was in the city too. Those two things had to be tied together—the verbal threat that there would be consequences and then the follow-through with them after not having easy access to what he'd demanded. After all, he knew enough about what I worked on to make demands.

The next few hours would be full of answering questions. I was looking forward to going home and running my theory about what lay behind the attack with Trev.

"I'll go get your antibiotics filled at the pharmacy," Peter said with an assuring smile.

"No, it's fine. I'll do it on the way home." There was no way would I let anyone else have access to something I ingested, even if it was just Peter.

Sandy gasped, and I looked up to see Trev barreling into the room. Gone was the laid-back guy. Holy hell—if I hadn't known him, I would have been terrified. His face was taut, his eyes blazed retribution, and a muscle jumped along his jawline. He didn't even spare Sandy a glance—his gaze seared me with laser-like focus.

With each step he took toward me, my heart rate kicked up a notch. As he neared, the fear that clung to me like static fizzled away. He stopped in front of me, bent to my ear, and whispered, "We'll talk privately."

I shivered in response. With that one phrase, the weight of my hypothesis eased. I understood what he meant. We would tell the police the facts and discuss our theories in private. There was too much at stake with the military vector and the dealings with the Russian laboratory. I could wait, even if the next few hours dragged.

Two and a half hours later and with an official report filed, I was buckled into Trev's SUV and headed for home. I was exhausted. We'd already picked up my prescription that would ensure the anthrax spores didn't germinate.

Trev took his gaze off the road for a split second. "So, anthrax."

"Yes." I shifted so my back leaned against the passenger door. "I think this may tie into the man who wants the military vector. I don't think he's related to that program or anyone in it."

"I don't, either. We've turned over every stone imaginable, and none have yielded results. We're digging deeper into people who have access to your work. Zen Pharmaceuticals, the Russian lab, and your colleagues in-house."

My top teeth sank into my bottom lip, and I rolled it back and forth. "I think the anthrax was meant to tie together the man who pushed me and pulled me into the alleyway near my office. Remember I told you he said if I didn't follow through with giving him the vector, there'd be consequences I wouldn't like?"

"Yes," he growled.

"Well, there was a note stuck over whatever word was origi-nally on the inside of the card. It said, 'consequences,' which seems like it came from him." I was trying hard to stay calm, but it wasn't working too well. I held Trev's gaze. "When you're with me at home, I feel safe. I don't think he can get to me then. And at work, the windows of opportunities for him to have physical access have shrunk unless he somehow gains entrance past building security. Which won't happen."

"I agree that your attacker is the likeliest suspect with the anthrax incident. If I could get my hands on him, we'd know why he's targeting you and if there is an even bigger threat out there."

"I think it's him." The other threat… I had a horrible sense it was something inside me, but I wasn't going there. It wasn't something I was ready to face just yet. "We had an anthrax scare when four envelopes were delivered to people in Washington, but I don't think this is the same sort of thing. My guess is that it's personal and connects to Russia."

"I'm following you." Trev turned the corner, and my home came into view.

"In 2016, there was an anthrax outbreak when the layers of permafrost thawed, releasing spores from dead reindeer. It was a remote area, so it wasn't a widespread epidemic." It felt important, and I had to share it with him. "If I'm remembering correctly, a child died, and dozens were infected. I feel like it's the same guy. Could he be pointing us there? I'm not sure why he's after me, but I think that's our best chance to find out who he is."

THE SUN SLIPPED PAST THE horizon, taking with it the brilliant splashes of orange and red across the ocean. While fear clung to the edges of my awareness, I craved a light evening—I wanted to laugh. I warned Trev that I needed a mental hiatus, at least for the night. He seemed to understand.

A pan banged behind me, and I left the bay window that overlooked the beach, trying to shake the fear from the prior break-in attempt. My stalker was getting braver, and I was grateful for Trev's presence but not so much that the mess that he was cleaning up in my kitchen, and quite possibly making more of, didn't matter.

I took a few steps closer, and I couldn't help but laugh. The pans not stacked in the sink lay scattered across the counter. A spaghetti noodle was hanging in his hair. I plucked it from amidst strands of blond then put water on the corner of a dishtowel. I wiped with the wet part of the towel onto where sauce had splattered in his hair before running my fingers along the side of his head, checking for any more. "You don't wear it down much," I said, commenting on his man bun, something I used to think was stupid, at least until I got a good look at Trev for the first time. It was uncanny how much he looked like Ben Dahlhaus.

"I need to cut it," he said.

I leaned a hip against the counter so I could see his face better. "Because of your job?" I knew he was a former Navy SEAL, but I didn't think his current career would have such stipulations.

"No. Well, it's easier to have it short when going on missions, but that's not why."

I waited, toying with the stem of my wineglass. "And… the reason is?"

He smirked. "It's long from a little bit of laziness and embracing the wannabe life of a surfer."

He was sexy as hell. "You surf?" I couldn't stop picturing him riding the waves.

"Some. When there's downtime."

Shadows swam in his eyes, his laid-back demeanor slipped, and I wondered what I was missing. "Do you not like your job?"

He stacked another dish in the dishwasher. "I do. I'm lucky.

I get to work with my brother and guys who have been more of a family than Chris and I ever had. I wouldn't change it for anything."

"Then what is it?" I laid my hand on his bicep. My question was met with silence. His shrug was the only response I got.

He always gave off the impression of not having a care in the world unless he was working on security or making sure I was safe. But I had gotten to know him, and I could see his layers and that they hid the pain. His laid-back persona masked turmoil from his younger years. Even though he'd shared a great deal with me, I felt there was more, and it was something dark.

SEVENTEEN

TREV

THE CAR JERKED TO A halt, and I was out the door and rounding the bumper before Jules said hello. A quick visual scan of our surroundings was all I was able to accomplish before I wrapped my arm around her shoulders. "What are you doing waiting out here? You should be inside with the security guard until I pull up."

"Nothing will happen to me." A smile played around her red lips, and mischief flashed in her eyes.

What's that about? She knew the risks, especially after she was grabbed into an alley and threatened, and then the anthrax scare. I ushered her into the passenger seat then got into the driver's side and pulled away from her workplace. "Why are you taking off from work early? Everything good?"

Silence stretched between us, and I glanced her way. With her lips pursed, her gaze crawled over me. My body responded. I focused back on the road and not on her roaming eyes. She was being strange. Worry clawed at me over the shift in her demeanor while we waited for the light to change. We'd had a great night talking, and after I'd dropped her at work that morning, I hadn't expected to be back until after five at the very earliest.

"Yep"—she popped the P—"everything's fine. I decided to cut out early. It's a gorgeous day, and staying inside to work on formulas wasn't how I wanted to spend it."

I risked another glance at her. The Jules I knew was a borderline workaholic. "Sure you're feeling okay?"

Her husky laugh filled the car, but instead of its usual heady effect, chills skated along my spine. Something was off. It had to be the challenge of finding her footing without her assistant. Then the scare from the attack and the anthrax.

"Never better." She shifted closer, and her fingers tiptoed up my forearm until they curled around my bicep. "I can think of something we could do this afternoon."

I pulled into the driveway of her small house on the beach. After helping her out of the vehicle, I took her keys and unlocked the front door. "Wait here."

When I was positive she was going to stay by the door, I walked the house to make sure no one was waiting inside. I didn't think anyone would be, but I wasn't going to miss doing something so important, especially because I had to run out and leave her there alone. My phone had been going off nonstop, and I had to take care of a few things for Chris, Liam, and Hawk—our team was stretched thin. Most of the guys were out on missions. Connor was with me, but not on-site yet. I would have him take over night duty and remain invisible to Jules, though he was a much-needed part of ensuring her safety.

I rounded the corner and made my way back to the front of the house. God, she was gorgeous. She leaned against the door, and her dark-brown hair was pushed behind one shoulder with a long, thick wave of it covering her left eye. With her chin tipped down, she looked at me beneath sooty lashes. She lifted her hand and shoved the hair from her face, and the tiny charms of her bracelet slipped from the cuff of her sweater and jingled as she moved.

"I have to take care of a job, but I'll be back soon."

Her gray-and-black skirt swirled around her ankles as she shifted, baring a small flash of her flat midriff above the waist-line. I wanted to tease her skin as I pulled her close. My cell buzzed. What I was about to do went against everything I was comfortable with, but it would only be for an hour, and I had the cameras all set up outside and a hired security detail keeping an eye on the place.

"Since you're leaving for a while, we should go out to eat tonight. I don't feel like cooking." She closed the distance between us so only a whisper of space remained. Her finger trailed down my arm. She rose to her toes and pressed a kiss to my mouth, her tongue darting out along my lower lip before she stepped back. "Hurry back."

A stirring of desire warred with my need to leave, and I leveled her with a stern expression. "Stay inside."

A slow smile spread across her lips. "I'll be waiting for you."

EIGHTEEN

THE ERRAND I HAD TO run for Chris took a full hour. I hated leaving Jules alone for that long, but I had two security guards watching her house—otherwise, I never would have gone. She didn't know about them and didn't need to. If anything happened while I was away, I trusted the men I'd left in charge. Besides, Connor had arrived early and was watching the back of her lot. Why he couldn't talk with the ancestry-company owner about whatever mission Keegan was on was beyond me, but Chris had his reasons.

After ringing the doorbell, I stood back so she could see it was me through the custom crescent-moon window on the front door. It was one of the more unique doors I'd seen, and it fit her personality. Even though Jules was a genetic epidemiologist, she had an ethereal, dreamy side to her.

Maybe we can walk down the beach and grab hot dogs or something. She'd wanted to go out, but I couldn't stop thinking of the meals she'd cooked for me. That's what I wanted, some amazing Italian food. My mouth watered. Dating her could become a problem if I didn't run daily. I could easily gain weight from how much she'd fed me over the past few weeks.

The door opened, and Jules stood there in white capris and a red top. I didn't know which I liked her in better, the skirt from earlier or the way the pants and shirt hugged her curves.

"Is everything okay?" Her brows furrowed.

"Yep. Sorry that took so long. I hoped I'd be back in a half hour."

"Oh." She stepped aside and swung the door wider. The smell of sauce on the stove hit my nose. "It's fine. I haven't been here long."

My fingers closed around her arm, and I turned her back to me. "What? I asked you to stay inside."

She frowned, confusion swimming in her eyes. "How else was I supposed to get home? I had to go outside in order to leave the building."

"Well…" My stomach growled. "You decided to cook rather than go out?"

Her head knocked back, and a small laugh escaped her lips. "Why would I want to go out to dinner?"

What the hell is going on? "You said you wanted to go out to eat earlier."

"Yeah, no…" She shook her head and continued to the kitchen.

"Are you sure you're okay? You seemed a little off earlier—"

"Oh, yeah. I'm fine, just had a tough time at work today finishing up some projects that Fran and I were involved on."

I followed. Jules went straight to the stove and stirred the sauce. My stomach growled, and she laughed. "What can I do to help?"

"Nothing. The pasta is already draining in the sink. Go sit down. It'll be ready in a few minutes."

I dropped onto a kitchen chair and leaned back, watching the graceful way Jules moved from the stove to the pantry. She came back with two big bowls. There was an innate kindness to her that radiated through her fluid movements. Her behavior earlier was so odd, but she must have been trying to bury her emotions with physicality. Jules had been aggressive toward me, which I welcomed, but she'd never behaved so brazenly. It was a strange shift in her character, even in her mannerisms. While grief had many stages—and I'd also gone through many when I thought my brother was dead—I wasn't sure how I felt about the instability I'd witnessed in her moods today.

I stood and went to help, wanting to do what I could to make the day better for her. When I reached for one of the bowls she held, our hands touched. Her gorgeous face tilted to mine, and the smile she wore nearly brought me to my knees. There was a sweetness about her I was drawn to. Within all the ugliness of life, someone like her was a gift meant to be cherished.

Dinner was over before I knew it, and the sinking sun ushered in the night. The guards would have been relieved by new ones. "Is there anything you want to do tonight?"

She set her wineglass down and toyed with the stem before looking at me with hooded eyelids. I worked on the dishes since she'd cooked. "We could pick up where things left off last night."

I couldn't help but tease her. "Netflix?"

Heat colored her cheeks.

I chuckled. I didn't know how much longer I could go without touching her.

"I was hoping that show wasn't what you were talking about."

After the last dish had been put away, I linked our fingers and pulled her out of the kitchen and down the hall.

Amusement played around the upturned corners of her mouth even as her eyes dilated. I couldn't get enough of her. I wanted everything.

"Wait." She nibbled on her lower lip. "I'll just be a minute."

She slipped into the master bathroom, and a second later, I heard the sink running. I prowled the room, making sure the shades didn't allow anyone to see inside. I passed by her dresser when a flash of silver caught my eye. I bent and retrieved the bracelet I'd seen Jules wear earlier today. A link was broken. It must have snagged on something and fallen when she'd changed out of her skirt.

The door opened, and every nerve in my body sprung taut. The bracelet slid from my hand to land in a forgotten tangle on her dresser. "What's wrong?"

Her olive-toned skin was pale, and she pressed her lips so tightly together that the rosy color was leached from them. "I…" She swayed on her feet.

I rushed to her side. Grasping her arms, I led her to sit on the bed.

She shook her head. "I don't know. It was weird."

I sat next to her and moved my thumbs in soothing circles over her hands. "I won't think so. Tell me."

"I—I was washing my face, and when I looked in the mirror, there was this odd duality. I was staring at my reflection, but it wasn't my reflection. I don't know how to describe it."

I pressed a kiss to her forehead. I didn't know what she meant, but I wanted to double-check the bathroom to be sure. After all, there was a window in there. "Stay here." I left her sitting on the edge of the bed. I flicked the light on and was met with white shiplap, a claw-foot tub, a clean vanity, and a large shower. Nothing was out of place, and the blinds were drawn over the single pane. I checked the lock to ensure it was secure. It was.

When I came out, she was running her hand over the T-shaped scar on the inside of her arm. "Nothing, right?"

I shook my head then took her in my arms. "Doesn't mean you were wrong. Maybe you sensed someone outside the window or were startled for a moment. It happens. Try not to worry too much." It was odd timing but something I'd just realized, so I voiced it. "You don't have any other mirrors in the house."

She shook her head. "No. My mom noticed I'd get headaches often and traced the issue to memory fragments I remembered while looking in the mirror. She took them down."

It made sense. Given how she'd described their relationship, I could imagine her mom doing that to eliminate Jules's distress.

We stayed upright on the bed for several moments with her head tucked under my chin. I ran my hand through her silky hair, my heart breaking for her. She'd been through so much from the stalker, to someone messing with her at the office, to Fran's death, and an anthrax scare. It was no wonder that she was on edge.

She shifted and dropped her head to my shoulder, tilting her chin until our gazes collided. *Goddamn.* Lust slammed into me at the smoldering desire reflected in her parted lips and dilated pupils.

I took her mouth in a hungry kiss. My fingers curled in the thick hair at the back of her head. A soft moan escaped as my tongue tangled with hers. Sparks of electricity shot through my body at the feel of her silky skin and responsive reactions. I deepened the kiss then lay her back on the bed, following her down.

Her hands roved over my back, slipping under my shirt. I lifted up enough to pull it over my head, tossing it aside. I cupped her hip before inching along her side to her stomach. Soft, inviting skin notched my need higher. Each time she wiggled under me, arching her back, my need for her got more and more out of control.

Being with her was all-consuming, causing tunnel vision. I had one goal, and she was it. Nothing else mattered. My mind went fuzzy, and desire took over. I didn't know what it was about her, but I knew my connection to her was dangerous. My job was to keep her safe, but all I could think about was her and the things I wanted to do to her.

The button on her pants popped open with a flick of my thumb, and I eased the zipper down.

She nudged my hands away, and I shifted to my side, giving her room as she shimmied out of them.

"You're killing me, Jules."

She flopped back on the bed, her hair splayed over the pillow, and gave me the sexiest smile before tugging on my arm. I covered her again, pressing kisses along her neck, over her collarbone, and to the gentle swell of her—

Blaring sound screamed through the room in short blasts, interrupting what we were about to do. *Shit.* I jumped off her, reaching for the gun I'd set on the side table. There was no reason for the fire alarm to go off.

Jules's eyes were wide as she'd grabbed for her pants. "I turned the stove off. I don't understand."

There was no smell of smoke. Even though I wanted her to stay in the bedroom, there were windows someone could break through if they made it past the guards. My phone buzzed in my pocket, and I slipped an earpiece in, connecting it with a tap of a button.

"No movement outside. No visible flames or smoke," Connor reported.

"Could be a faulty battery," I answered. The line fell silent. He would have known that I was checking the interior, and I knew they were doing the same outside.

Jules hooked a finger through a belt loop in the back of my jeans. That worked for me. I liked knowing she was close and that no one could get to her without going through me first, which wouldn't happen.

In a matter of seconds, we were standing in her kitchen, staring at the lone lit candle on the table. *What the hell is going on?* It was small and wouldn't have caused the fire alarm to go off. It was beyond strange, and when I turned to her, my gut clenched tight at her fearful expression.

Her lower lip trembled slightly, and she wrung her hands. "I swear I blew that out."

NINETEEN

I EASED MY ARM OUT from under Jules, who cuddled against my side. I slid from the bed and pulled on my jeans under the light from the silvery moon. I needed to talk with Connor and had sent him a text. I slipped out the sliding door and waited on the patio for him to emerge from the trees on the left.

I was too restless to remain in the same bed with her—I didn't want to wake her, especially since it'd taken her so long to fall asleep. We'd talked about the candle and how it spoke volumes that something wasn't right. But I kept wondering how someone could have gotten inside. And why was the candle significant? I drummed my fingers against my thigh.

Not even a noise sounded before Connor dropped onto the chair next to mine. While our core team hadn't grown up with Connor, he'd become one of us while we were active duty, and he had our backs with the same unwavering dedication and ferocity that we all shared. I appreciated his palpable predatory presence, but I was exhausted, and it was adding an edginess that I knew would keep me awake for the rest of the night. "You need to tone down the menace."

His response was a chuckle. We balanced each other in a sort of good-cop-bad-cop vibe, but we were soldiers rather than police. I was grasping for analogies in my exhaustion.

"There were footprints that couldn't have been from you or

Jules found at the edge of her property yesterday. I've stationed a guy to cover the area near the beach."

"Anything you noticed around the time the fire alarm went off?"

"No. Not on our end. You and Jules were the only ones on the property."

"Something isn't adding up."

"You said it was from a candle. That shouldn't have been enough to set off the alarm unless it was faulty." A beat of silence hung. "Jules said she blew it out, right? Did you see her do this?"

"That's what's eating at me. I didn't. I've seen firsthand how preoccupied she can be." I pushed my hair off my forehead and held it for a moment, tugging at the roots. "I don't know. She swore she remembers blowing out the candle and is sure someone got inside."

"Could be a coincidence."

"Too many of those." They were adding up. "My gut says we're headed for trouble. The Russian doctor knowing about the restricted military vector is a huge red flag. His knowledge must come either from personnel who know about the tool kit or colleagues she works with. We need to take a closer look at the scientists."

"I agree—and their family and friends." Connor stood. "Get some sleep. I've increased the security from two to four. Nothing will get past them."

I hoped so. "It would help if we had our guys here." Mike and Hayden were with Matt and Jo, working on another assignment. Jack, Keegan, Hawk, and Chris were engaged in yet another one that I didn't have a single detail about, and Liam was helping them. Connor was the only one on our team who had been free enough to come here physically. Having him lead the security helped to take my mind off it and stay focused on Jules instead.

"I agree. These guys have been vetted. They'll do the job

we need them to." His heavy hand landed on my shoulder. "Get some sleep."

If my mind would turn off, I would.

⁂

JULES

TREV BACKED THE SUV DOWN the driveway while I stared out the passenger window, humiliated. If there was something that could go wrong, it had. Aside from the lit candle, there had been nothing burning in the house the night before, and the candle wouldn't have been enough to set off the alarm. Trev said it had to be faulty. He would have it replaced.

It wasn't only that. I'd woken late when my alarm didn't go off. Alone. Trev had slept in the other room. He'd said he had to stay alert and couldn't do that with me lying by his side. It felt like a rejection even though he was doing his job. I got it, but still.

There was more that bothered me. My bedside clock wasn't working. It'd stopped at 7:16, and the time had left me uneasy. I have no idea why. My head throbbed with pain just behind my eyes. Something about that exact time felt as though it held significance. Paranoia pinged through me at odd times during the day, and it currently had me in a tight grip.

"Hey." Trev squeezed my thigh before returning his hand to the wheel. "You okay?"

"Yep. Tired, I guess." My practically throwing myself at him last night and then nothing happening was embarrassing enough, so I wasn't about to mention any additional insecurities to him. I had to be careful. I got that. The problem was that I wasn't always positive I wasn't at fault, and I tried to bring anything that was cause for concern to Trev's attention. "Turn up ahead. The dry cleaner is on the right."

He turned where I'd indicated. "Since it's Saturday, we should do something fun."

Sure… Did he miss the memo that I was where fun went to die? "What were you thinking?"

"Let's pack a lunch and head to the harbor. We can go out on the boat, spend a few hours on the water. It'll be relaxing."

Instant tension settled between my shoulder blades, and I glanced out his window at the miles of ocean to the left. Sunlight glinted off the water. It didn't look too choppy, but given how things had been going for me, I didn't think I had it in me to go out on the water. With my luck, I would agree, and then a storm would roll in while we were at sea. "I'd rather not."

"Okay. Let's go for a walk on the beach instead."

There wasn't a trace of annoyance in his voice, and I relaxed back in my seat. "I'd like that."

He pulled into the strip mall that housed my dry cleaner. I jumped out of the car. "I'll be right back."

The sound of his door opening made me pause, and I caught the look of amusement on his face.

"I can go into the cleaners, Trev. Nothing will happen."

"I don't want to sit in the car." He grinned.

I rolled my eyes. *Sure, that's why he's walking with me.* His hand settled on the small of my back. It felt right. A tiny bit of embarrassment over yesterday slid away.

The bell jingled overhead as we entered the humid shop. We stood behind the two people standing in line. Rummaging around in my purse, I found the slip for my clothes. The woman in front of us kept turning around and sneaking glances at Trev. I grinned. I didn't blame her. He was gorgeous, even more since I'd gotten to know him better. *I've fallen hard for him.*

I stumbled as we moved forward and realized the truth behind that thought. Trev clutched my hip, pulling me to his side to steady me. I leaned into him as my heart pounded like a desperate inmate in an attempt to break free from my rib cage.

His hand curled around me, and he held me against him even as the woman snuck another look at him. I caught the tight set of her lips as she saw our new position, and I wanted to laugh. She was next. In no time at all, probably because she didn't see an opening to hit on Trev, it was our turn.

After I handed over my receipt, the clerk retrieved my dry cleaning then hung it on the bar next to the counter. Trev grabbed my clothes for me while I paid. We went back to the SUV, and my mind spun with how to handle the fact that I cared about him—a lot. A slight breeze rustled my hair, and I tucked it behind my ears. Key fob in hand, he unlocked the truck, opened the door for me, then secured my clothes on a hook over the side window in the back. *A girl could get used to this.*

It wasn't a far drive, and we were back at my house in record time. "I'll just be a minute," I called over my shoulder to Trev. I wanted to hang up my clothes. I tore the plastic covering off and turned. *Wait.* I ran my hand over the clothes. I swore there were a few tops that should've been there, and my favorite black-and-gray skirt wasn't in the batch, either. I'd wanted to wear that to work on Monday. I flipped through the clothes, searching for the missing items. Maybe I'd misplaced them or they'd gotten lost at the cleaners.

A tremor shook my hand before I shut my closet doors. There were too many coincidences and things that didn't add up. A heavy weight settled over my heart. There had to be an explanation. I thought about the letter from my mom, but still saw no real reason to open it—I wasn't in unknown danger. Everything could be easily explained. *Right?*

I'm not going crazy. Thinking it didn't ease my fears. It sure as hell felt like I was.

THE SCENT OF LASAGNA STILL filled the kitchen, and I sighed with satisfaction, the dry-cleaning worry from earlier today a distant memory. The clothes would turn up—they always did. We'd stuffed ourselves, and I needed to move around after such a big meal. Trev and I were doing the dishes before we went for a walk on the beach. With the windows open, the sound of the waves breaking against the shore lured us outside.

I was glad we'd checked the weather, and more so that I'd declined his offer of going out on the boat—a storm was coming through. A chill at the thought of being on the water skated over my skin. I couldn't think about it and was grateful when Trev spoke, distracting me. "We could leave some of the cleanup for later."

That was crazy talk, and I rolled my eyes despite the goose bumps that danced along my skin when his hand settled on the curve of my hip. "You know I like the kitchen cleaned up right away. There's nothing worse than coming back to a huge mess."

A wide grin spread across his sinfully kissable mouth. "You're right. I can think of something else I'd rather do later."

He brushed my hair from my neck and pressed kisses down to my shoulder. "Stop." I couldn't help the giggle. "This is the last of the dishes, and then we're getting out of the house." His touch made it so I didn't want to leave.

"You want this back on the shelf in the living room?"

I craned my neck to see what he was talking about. "Yes, thanks." My mom's recipe book was in his hands, and anxiety shot through my blood. I could see the corner of her letter peeking out from the top of the binder, taunting me. Once more, the odd sense of dread pooled in my gut. I had the sinking sensation that I would be reading it sooner rather than later. Something would push me over the edge, and I had a feeling that what I'd thought had been a coincidence wasn't.

I closed the dishwasher and hung the dish towel. I needed to get out of there. With the storm still a ways away, I wanted to take advantage of the beach. "Ready?"

Trev tangled his fingers with mine as we went out the back door. The air was charged with the expectancy of the pending bad weather, and our pace down the walkway to the shore quickened. Wind pushed my hair back from my face, and I dropped his hand for a second to tie it back.

"You've been tense, more so than usual." He tugged my hand after my hair was secured, pulling me closer.

I watched the tremulous shoreline. Waves broke against the sandy embankment only to retreat into the churning mass of building swells. Then the process started all over again. Shells lay scattered along the coastline, and come morning, there would be new treasures to be found. The repetitive motion and soothing sounds did a lot to relax the tension residing between my shoulders and pounding in my temples. I let the oddities of the events over the past few days swirl in my mind before I would lay them at Trev's feet. He waited for me to tell him what was wrong. I needed to, especially on the off chance that they were nothing. "I guess I've been stressed."

"I understand why, but is there anything else that's bothering you?" He gave my hand a gentle squeeze. "You know that it's not insignificant, whatever it is. I need and want to know."

"I feel strange even telling you because it's probably grief and anger over Fran's death. She wouldn't have killed herself—I can't accept that. That's the main issue. Then—it's stupid." I hung my head, frustrated.

"Jules, tell me." He hooked his finger under my chin, tipping my face up to meet his gaze.

I pushed out a breath then dove straight to the most recent worry. "My clock stopped at 7:16 today and at that same time yesterday."

He pressed his lips into a tight line. "Trust me, that bothered me as well and is something I'm investigating further."

"It's so random, and I'm constantly feeling like I'm going crazy. I mean, I picked up my dry cleaning and swore I was missing a skirt and two tops. When I called to check, they said I'd gotten them the last time." I dragged my teeth over my bottom lip. "I don't remember. It's all building, these silly issues, and I can't make sense of it." It wasn't the first time in my life that I'd felt that way. When the memories from before the accident tried to return, reality seemed to fragment, and I didn't always trust myself. Part of me wondered if the majority of the things happening, like the candle and my things being moved, weren't because of that.

He tugged my hand and turned me to him, the water behind his back. "You've had a lot happen. You're allowed to worry. As for the dry cleaning, we'll look for the clothes."

I pushed up to my tiptoes and pressed a kiss to his mouth, a sense of lightness filling me since he'd acknowledged my fears. "Thank you."

He tucked a piece of hair that'd come loose behind my ear. "I want to know about what's bothering you."

God, he was killing me. With a small smile, I nodded, agreeing that'd I would tell him.

He winked, and butterflies took flight in my abdomen. "Let's walk to the pier and back. Then I guess I'll let you talk me into sitting through that weird series you like on Netflix."

I laughed. "You can pretend you don't like it, but I won't believe you. You're totally into it."

"Lies!"

He nudged me to resume our walk, and I swatted his arm. It was rock-solid, which wasn't unusual. Alarm screamed through my veins at the stony expression that came over his face, the one reserved for when he was on guard or there was trouble approaching. I glanced ahead as Trev shifted me to his other side so I was between him and the water.

A man jogged down the beach toward us. Heavily muscled, he wore a pair of shorts and a baseball hat pulled down to shield his face. He was the first person we'd come across—the ominous weather kept most away.

Still, it wasn't unusual for someone to jog along the beach. What set my internal alarms blaring was the man's build. Fit as the military men I'd administered injections to, he was tall with deeply tanned skin. It was in the way he moved, his height, how he carried himself, and the aura around him, which was dangerous. I couldn't place him. Even so, a sense of familiarity flooded my mind.

Trev dropped my hand, his body taut. I knew he would spring into action at a second's notice should he need to. *Please don't need to.* Fear clawed at my mind. *Could that be the same man who'd grabbed me not once, but twice?*

The sound of his gym shoes hitting the sand was lost in the roar of the waves. The man's head was down as he neared. A chill swept over me. Trev was tense beside me, and as the guy jogged by, he lifted his gaze to mine. *Holy shit.*

Intense brown eyes bore into me, and I got the unmistakable sense he meant me harm. Trev pivoted on his heel and went after the guy while my entire body shook. It had to be the one who'd attacked and threatened me in the alley.

Rooted to the same spot on the shoreline, I wrapped my arms around my chest as Trev grabbed the jogger's arm and turned him around. Angry voices rode the wind, one accusatory and the other full of denial.

My mind whirled. I was aware that Trev and his team didn't think my attacker was anyone in the program regarding the tool kit. He had let it slip that the attacker could have been someone associated with one of the military guys, which was frightening, as the chance of catching an outsider was lower. That was a problem I wasn't going to worry about. There was no doubt in my mind that Trev would have my back. He'd just proven it.

Another man raced down the beach from the direction of my house and joined the discussion. After a few more minutes, Trev returned to my side.

"Is it him?" *Please let this be over.*

"He's denying he knows you or has crossed paths with you before. The guard will detain him, and Connor will check what he's said to find the truth."

Another guard joined the first, and we cast a wide berth around them and the jogger as we made our way back to my house.

"I want you back inside." His grip was viselike without hurting. "We'll know more in a few minutes. There's a chance it's the same guy."

We made it back and slipped through the sliding doors to my kitchen, where I fell into a chair to wait for news. There was a chance that it would all be over after they questioned him… or not.

TWENTY-ONE

TREV

Wispy clouds feathered the blue sky, and a gentle breeze ruffled Jules's hair. "You sure you want to do this?" I paused, trying to read her expression. After yesterday's jogger incident, I was surprised she wanted to go near the beach. He'd shaken her up. I'd texted Connor and had him detain the man until we learned more. We ran his information, but nothing came up. There was no reason to hold him. Even so, something didn't add up with the way he'd looked at her.

"Of course I do." Her red lips curved into a smile. "It's a beautiful day, and I want to hang out with you on the water."

Not even an hour after I'd left her at work, she'd called and asked me to pick her back up. The weather was unseasonably warm, and she'd said there was no way she could stay inside when it was so nice out and suggested going out on my boat. I'd almost dropped the phone. It was the first time she'd shown an enthusiastic willingness to go out on the water. I wanted to question her odd behavior but was too happy to take her out. She needed to be able to safely have fun and relieve some stress.

Her fingers curled around my extended hand, and I helped

her on board. I'd toyed with moving my boat to Maine and joining most of my team. Building a house on the immense amount of property we'd all pooled together to buy for just such a reason was tempting. I wasn't the only one holding out, though—Connor and Hayden lived in California. And since I'd met Jules, I wasn't sure it would be in the cards for me to move.

After untying the ropes of my high-performance speedboat, I pushed away from the dock. Jules moved to the chair next to the captain's seat, and I got us moving at a slow clip out of the no-wake canal. A few minutes later, I was able to open up the motor. A wide smile stretched across her face, and I found myself grinning as well. Whatever caused her to overcome her fears of being out in the deep water and on a boat was fine with me. I wouldn't push the issue.

"Go faster!" she shouted over the sound of the motor and sea spray as we cut through the swells.

I increased our speed. The front end of the boat sliced through waves and slammed into the larger ones. A carefree laugh drew my gaze again. God, she was beautiful.

Forty-five minutes later, I dropped anchor at her request. I'd planned to go for a short ride and head back in. Last time when we had been on a boat together, aside from our dinner under the stars, she'd gotten pretty freaked out.

Sun glinted off the water, and the boat rocked and swayed. I pulled two waters from the cooler and handed her one. A mischievous sparkle lit her eyes.

"Let's go for a swim." She winked before standing and shimmying out of her tiny white shorts. The teal sweater was next, her bracelet jingling with each move. I stood as she tossed her white silk panties and bra in the growing pile of clothes.

Shit. I tore off my shirt and shoved my jeans down as she dove into the water. When I surfaced, she ducked under until she came up inches from me. I snaked my hands around her and drew her close. Goddamn, she felt amazing, her soft, silky skin sliding along mine. While treading water, I dipped my head to hers and kissed her. Her legs wrapped around my waist, and her arms clung to my neck in a tight squeeze. I almost pulled away, concerned that she was panicking in the water, until her tongue plunged into my mouth and all thought left my brain.

Water splashed up to our chins, and I released her mouth. Kissing in the water wasn't exactly easy, and that's all we could do in deep water. "Maybe we should go back in the boat."

"I want to swim." She grinned before ducking out of my arms and taking off at a fast freestyle away from the boat.

Who the hell is this woman? For a few seconds, I watched her confident strokes before taking off after her. My mind continued to puzzle over the change in her behavior and the almost bitter taste in my mouth. I let her get a head start then dove in after her. We had at least an hour before she said she had to get back to work. I wasn't going to waste a second of it.

TWENTY-TWO

FOR THE FIFTH TIME, I glanced at the clock. The day had dragged since Trev had dropped me off, even with all the work to do to prepare the next military dosage. I'd tweaked the vector and wanted to run a few more tests before we left for Washington at the end of the week.

Peter shifted, and I caught a glimpse of his monitor. Goose bumps broke out across my skin. "What are you doing?"

He turned to me, his thick brows furrowed. "Answering Dr. Mikhailov's questions about whether we learned who was responsible for the anthrax attack."

"No." I shook my head adamantly. "You cannot update him or anyone there about what's happened here. Were you not paying attention in the meeting?" I ran my hand over my forehead in an attempt to relieve the tension. Fran would've been on top of things. Peter wasn't working out. Plus, I'd caught him digging through some of my past work, studying the calculations, tests, and results. I didn't like it and had confronted him. He'd claimed he was curious and wanted to familiarize himself with past work to better anticipate how to work with me. Something about his reasoning rang as odd to me, but I couldn't think of why I should bring it to Carl's atten-tion. Peter frowned, his lips in a thin line, and my irritation spiked even higher.

"I wasn't in that meeting. Remember?"

Oh, shoot. This is on me, at least sort of. He'd come in late *again,* and the tasks I had to have him finish before the meeting hadn't been addressed. I'd set him to those instead when he'd strolled in. "That's right. You were chasing after the FDA person to ensure this last batch would be tested immediately when I'm done with it." *Still…* "Didn't Carl pull you into the office to give you a summary of what we talked about?" I swore he'd said he would when I told him where Peter was.

He leaned back in his chair and crossed his arms over his thin chest. "No. Why don't you tell me."

I didn't like his attitude but couldn't really blame him for feeling out of the loop. It was a big deal. "After the anthrax incident, we were to stop all assistance with the Russian lab until further investigations are done." At least my conscience was clear—we'd ensured they had enough of the antibodies for those infected.

The defensive position he'd assumed fell away as his arms dropped down. "Wouldn't Dr. Mikhailov be aware that we cut off communications?"

I nodded.

"I get that we need to tighten security, but are we seriously assuming Russian scientists, whom we are helping, would attack us with anthrax?"

It did seem a little far-fetched, but not when we looked at some of the coincidences that had taken place. "While this particular anthrax wasn't proven to have come from Siberia, I'm sure you'll remember that an outbreak happened in the early twentieth century due to thawing permafrost. There are too many parallels pointing to an unknown threat from Russia. What have you shared with him?"

"Not much, at least nothing of significance. He only

contacted me this morning to ask about what had happened and if we'd learned about who was responsible for the attack."

"You need to let Carl know about this." After Peter left to do so, I couldn't stop thinking about all that had happened.

Where the leak about the restricted military vector came from continued to be a concern. I wasn't sure if my unknown attacker was from our military or someone from Russia. And if they'd been sent from overseas, the threat was bigger than we'd thought.

Peter popped back in, jarring me from my thoughts.

"Everything okay?"

His thin hair was mussed, as if he'd run his hands through it repeatedly. "Yes. Carl is aware of Dr. Mikhailov fishing for information. He said he'd confer with Rich Stevens, some CIA person. I'm going to get coffee."

"Okay." I didn't have too many problems with Peter, but if his agitated behavior continued, he wouldn't be a good fit for me to work with. A momentary jolt of panic sliced through me —*could Peter be part of the leak about our tool kit's vector? If Russia's goal is to gain unlimited access to the delta-32 injections, does that mean they plan to wield a bioweapon against the United States while their infiltrators are genetically protected?* I would have to talk to Trev about it.

A heavy weight landed on my shoulder, and I jumped in my chair, startled. My head tilted back to see whose hand rested there. *Carl.* The squeeze he gave me sent an uneasy jolt to my gut. Every time our paths had crossed that day, my boss had touched me. It was strange and not at all welcomed.

I clenched my teeth to keep from snapping at him then turned in my chair and pushed back a few inches so he was forced to drop his hand. "Something I can help you with, Carl?" *What is going on?* He'd never been anything but professional with me. I guessed it was possible that I was reading the exchange incorrectly.

He leaned against the edge of my desk, drumming his

fingers on the surface. Each tap sent my blood pressure higher. "I was thinking about our trip to Washington. Instead of flying in late Thursday, we could take off from here, after work today. That way, we'd gain a day and could go to dinner and a show."

I barely stopped my mouth from falling open. *Was he asking me out on a date?* We were flying nonstop. Leaving early Thursday morning gave us that night at a hotel, and then we would work all day Friday in DC. "What is this about? If you're asking me out, that's not in any way acceptable." I couldn't wrap my head around what was going on with him. "Where is this coming from?"

"I'm confused, Jules." He frowned. "You were the one who approached me about going early."

In whose reality? "No, Carl, I did not. And not only is it incredibly unprofessional and offensive that you'd imply I asked you—my boss—out on a date, but your attention today is unacceptable."

Confusion clouded his eyes as my voice rose in volume, drawing the notice of my colleagues. Good—they would be witnesses if Carl ever put me in a position like that again. It boggled my mind, as it wasn't typical of him. "I'll talk with Trev about when we leave for Washington. I believe he's flying us?" It really wasn't a question. He would be with me. I would make sure of it, and so would Trev.

Carl frowned. "No need to run anything by Trev."

"What about Dr. Mikhailov contacting Peter?"

"I've put a call into Rich. I plan to inform him so we're all on the same page."

That was good, I guessed. Why he didn't want me to check with Trev about flying out was odd, though. At least my anger had run its course. There was no way Carl would pull anything like that in the future, not if he wanted me to continue to work for him, and I knew for a fact he valued my contributions above all else.

"Another thing I wanted to confirm with you was replacing

Trev on the weekends. He can continue to drive you to and from work as we'd first arranged, but another company will monitor your house over the weekend."

"Why?" Alarm caused my back to straighten even more. "Trev works around my schedule, and I feel safe with him. I don't want to have to get to deal with someone else."

He knocked his knuckles against my desk twice. "We'll see. Let me know the results when you finish testing."

"Yeah, sure." *What the hell is going on with him?*

Pushing that crazy conversation from my mind, I got back to work. I glanced at my silent phone again, wondering why I hadn't heard from Trev at all. That wasn't normal. Shrugging, I vowed to calm down. *I'm sure he's busy.* With another peek at the clock, I texted him to tell him what time I would be out front.

Unlike the rest of the day, that last hour flew by. I pushed the heavy door open and stepped out on the sidewalk just as Trev pulled up to the curve. Exhaustion beat at me. He jogged around the car and opened my door. My eyes drifted shut as he resumed his seat behind the wheel.

"Tired?" he asked.

"Beyond so. I want to go home, put on pajamas, and have a glass of wine before I pass out."

"I'm sure. It was a long day. Fun, though."

I could hear the smile in his voice but was too exhausted to question him about why it was "fun." Maybe it was for him. I didn't want to get into it. Minimal effort was all I could manage at the moment.

We pulled up my driveway, and I dragged myself out of the SUV and up the pathway to my front door. I loved the little crescent-moon window in the door. It made it look like a fairy tale. Sometimes that's what I needed. I wanted off the roller-coaster ride of weirdness going on.

I put the key into the lock just as Trev spoke.

"How early do you want to go out on the boat tomorrow?"

My hand froze. I looked over my shoulder at him. "What are you talking about?"

His brows furrowed. "We talked about going out in the morning before work. Possibly swimming, if it isn't too cold."

What the hell? "I never said I'd go on the boat or swim out there." *First Carl's strange behavior, and now Trev?*

"Are you feeling okay?" Concern swam in his eyes as he reached out to caress my cheek.

I jerked my head back. I was sick of people telling me how I'd done or said something I never had. "No. I'm not," I snapped.

"What is going on, Jules?" His brows furrowed, and irritation tugged at the corners of his lips. "I'm getting whiplash with your mind games."

Mind games? Oh, no. I'm not going to put up with that. "I'm mentally and physically exhausted. I need a break tonight." I pushed the door open.

He took a step toward me, not even flashing his panty-melting grin. If he had, it would have helped his case. I held up my hand, palm out, and gentled my voice. "I'm going inside and crashing. *Alone.* I'll see you in the morning if you want to go for a run on the beach."

TWENTY-THREE

T HE SHRILL BEEP OF MY alarm pulled me from a ten-hour sleep, which I'd desperately needed. I slammed my hand down on the off button. I lazily blinked my eyes, willing them to focus, then turned on my side to get up.

A gentle breeze blew through my room, fluttering the curtains. I'd left the window cracked open, even though Trev hadn't slept over. I had no doubt he'd kept on eye on the house. Knowing he was out there enabled me to have a restful night—he just made me feel safe.

I pushed myself up and out of bed, letting the covers fall where they may. I needed to brush my teeth and splash some water on my face to wake up. I had another long day ahead of me, running tests in the lab, after I went for a run on the beach. I threw on shorts and a sports bra, ready to leave the bathroom when an image above the sink caught my eye. I paused. *Is there something in the mirror? Something out of place, that shouldn't be there?*

My heart rate picked up while I sucked in air and willed myself to look again. Ever since I could remember, I had a fear of mirrors—especially at night. I wasn't entirely sure why.

I was being a wimp. There wouldn't be anything unusual

there, but rational thought didn't matter. Dread held me rooted to the spot, and I struggled to turn my head and face the silvery surface. Ever since that morning when I'd seen something odd in the reflection, an irrational fear had danced on the outskirts of my consciousness. Taking a deep breath, I forced my gaze to the steamy mirror.

Holy hell. I sagged against the sink in relief. *It was nothing.* But when I turned halfway from the vanity, I swore I saw something else flit across the reflective surface. A hand had covered one of my own in a tight grip. A curtain of dark-brown hair obscured my face. Then there was the flash of a knife. I staggered backward. *It can't be real. My mind is playing tricks on me. God only knows why this is happening.* A brutal pain sliced my brain, followed by a lingering headache and a sudden realization of what the image was: my memories were trying to return.

I bent over the counter, turned the faucet on, and splashed my face with cold water. Even though my hands shook, I swore to myself that it wasn't real—with only a portion of the image, I didn't have the whole picture. I was tired or sleepwalking but also clearly not knowing what I'd lived through. For the time being, I would let it go, as I needed more of the memory to surface. With a finality that impressed even me, I dried my face and left the bathroom, not once checking the mirror again.

Struggling to dismiss what happened but forcing myself, I shoved my feet into my running shoes, exited the house, and made my way down to the beach. Air whooshed past my parted lips. Trev stood there, waiting. My shoulders dropped at least an inch, and the tension drained from them. *Everything will be okay.*

I gave him a small wave and kicked my pace up into a brisk jog. He matched my stride, taking the cues that I didn't want to talk. It was early, and I wanted to let the peacefulness of the morning sink in. There were so many questions and accusations about things that had not happened surrounding me that

I needed some space. Thankfully, he seemed to understand my unspoken plea for silence.

I matched him as he lengthened his stride and increased speed. My arms swung by my side, heels digging into the damp sand, and I pushed off with my toes. I felt my muscles straining as I fell into a welcome trancelike running zone beside him, our paces syncing as we raced to the pier two miles away.

Adrenaline fueled my body and helped to process the worry over testing, deadlines, and any potential threat when I would administer the next tool kit procedure.

The awkwardness with Peter worked to the forefront of my thoughts, and I briefly told Trev while we ran.

"I haven't been crazy about him working with you, either," he admitted. "So far, he's checked out, but I'm not comfortable with him."

We shifted to avoid a larger wave as it broke near our feet. "Okay. Thanks for checking up on him."

"We'll continue to keep an eye on him. Also, I disassembled your alarm clock to look for a trip wire or something that would stop the time at a certain number. I didn't find anything."

"That's good, I suppose." We fell back into silence as we increased the pace. I needed to get back and get ready for work, so we turned at the pier and headed back.

Our run was quick and exactly what I'd needed. In no time at all, I'd showered, eaten, and after Trev dropped me off, I buried myself in my work. The day that was supposed to drag, with monotonous tests and trials, flew by. I was packing up when Carl waved me into his office.

The door was open. He sat behind his desk in a white oxford and dark-red-and-navy-striped tie. Behind him, the blinds were partially closed over the large windows, effectively shielding my eyes from the sun. I stood there for a minute, but he didn't seem to notice me as he read a document. Rapping my knuckles against the doorjamb, I took a step inside. "You wanted to see me?"

"Juliana, yes. Please sit."

Alarm caused my hands to tremble. "What did you call me?"

His brows furrowed. "Your name. Is everything all right?"

"Why did you use my *full* name?" *No one did that. Ever. Not since Mom…*

"I wasn't aware that I did." He leaned back, and his chair squeaked. "Please sit. I'd like to talk to you about Trev."

I lowered myself into a chair across from him, my mind whirling from hearing "Juliana" on someone other than my mom's lips. It didn't feel right, and my world had tilted on its axis and was refusing to settle back.

"I've thought about what you said the other day and then again last night, and I went ahead and let Trev go. There haven't been any other incidents, and after his company looked into the military personnel that you'll be interacting with, I'm confident of your safety."

Panic shot through me, and I jerked forward in my chair so I was sitting on the edge of my seat. "What about the anthrax attack?"

"We've increased security in the building, and the mail is being screened."

"I don't know what you mean by 'last night.' Why would you let him go after I told you how much I didn't want to work with someone new? Now you're telling me there won't be anyone?" I clasped my hands in my lap to stop them from shaking, but no matter how hard I tried, I couldn't keep my voice from rising. "Where is this coming from?"

Carl frowned, and I noticed several heads swivel our way from the glass window separating his office from the rest of the lab. "Our discussion yesterday was completely different than what you're insinuating. You said yourself that there was no longer a need for a security detail and that everything that'd happened was either a coincidence or at the very least over with."

I shot to my feet. "No. I never said any of those things." Maybe I had chalked everything up to coincidence at one point, but that was in the very beginning.

Carl frowned. "Are you okay, Jules?"

I slammed my lips together to avoid inadvertently telling him precisely what I was feeling at the moment. After taking several deep breaths through my nose, I felt marginally calmer. "Not really, Carl. I'm going home. We can talk about this again in the morning." With that, I pivoted on my heel and walked out of his office. *Would he still be going to DC early?* I brushed the question aside. I didn't want to deal with him anymore.

I ducked my head as I passed by a few colleagues, who stared at me. It was none of their business.

With furious fingers, I texted Trev that I was ready to go. *Please be there.* I hoped he'd at least finish out the day and pick me up. My phone buzzed, and his response, *Already out front,* flooded me with relief.

"Have a good night, Dr. Moretti."

I absently waved at Josh, the security guard, as I rushed past the security desk and shoved the heavy door open. On the sidewalk, I didn't stop until I'd reached Trev. He was leaning against his Range Rover, a frown marring his face as soon as he saw me.

I dropped my gaze, and he stepped aside, opening the passenger door as he did so. I jumped inside, and he shut the door. Once he was seated too, he turned to me. *Please don't say you're quitting.* Before he spoke, I rushed forward with my idea. "I don't know why Carl decided to let you go, but I can pay you. I-I don't feel safe. Something strange is happening, and until we figure it out, I don't want to be alone." The thought of how Fran died flashed in my mind, and I realized how afraid I was. I needed him.

His large hand enveloped mine. "I didn't know what was

going on when Carl called me, especially after yesterday. But I hadn't planned on leaving you alone."

A tear rolled down my cheek, and I wiped it away, mortified. Not knowing what to say, I nodded.

"I'll be honest. I've gotten mixed signals from you lately, and I think we need to talk about what's going on." He rubbed the back of his neck. "Like the boat. One minute, you're terrified about being on it and in the deep water, and in the next, you're fearless."

Oh, God. That's part of the problem. "I honestly don't know what you're talking about. I feel like I'm going crazy, Trev. People keep telling me I did or said something that I didn't." I raised tear-filled eyes to meet his gaze. "Even you. Then I have these weird flashes when I look in the mirror. It's like a horror-show déjà vu moment that isn't real." I pushed up the sleeve of the lab coat I hadn't bothered to leave at work, exposing the scar on my inner arm. "There are times I look in the mirror and see myself staring back, but it doesn't exactly resemble me. And my scar"—my hand shook—"I've had a weird flash of the knife cutting, and I can't—"

"Shh." Trev drew me to him and wrapped me in his strong arms.

I couldn't hold back the tears. My body trembled while he held me tightly and whispered soothing words that I couldn't quite register. After a few minutes, I'd calmed enough to merely slump against him, my fisted hands loosening from the death grip I had on his shirt.

"What do you remember about a knife?"

I explained the vision. "It was just a flash of silver. Then the image was gone."

"So a portion of a memory?"

"Yes. Hopefully, I'll remember what it means soon."

"And then you got a headache?"

I nodded. A tremor went through me. "What Carl said…"

"I'm not going anywhere, and you're not paying me."

His hand continued to rub circles on my back, and I longed to fall asleep where I was. With reluctance, I disentangled myself and shifted back to face forward.

"Let's go to my place tonight. I think you need a change of scenery."

After I clicked my seat belt into place, he merged into traffic. While he drove, I stared unseeing out the window, wondering just what the hell was going on.

We traveled for about twenty minutes before he pulled up to what looked like luxury beachfront townhomes.

"This is your place?"

"Sure is." Trev got out, and I did the same.

I fell silent as we walked up the immaculately landscaped walkway. Through the glass panes framing the front door, I glimpsed a stunning view of the ocean through windows in the back of his home. He unlocked the door and held it open so I could walk in. The decor barely registered as I caught a glimpse of a turquoise cashmere top on the gray couch. With dread, I went over and plucked it from the back cushions. The marred spot, a chemical burn on the right sleeve, told me more than I wanted to know. I whirled around, the sweater extended before my body. "Why, when I've never been to your place before, is my sweater here?"

He shrugged and furrowed his brows. "You must have left it when we stopped here after boating and before I took you back to work."

"When?" I spoke through clenched teeth.

"When you wanted to take a few hours away from work and enjoy the sunshine." Trev ran his hands through his hair. "What's going on, Jules?"

I was done. Everyone around me was acting crazy. The back-and-forth argument would no doubt continue, but I wanted to be away from him for a while. There was no way I'd ever been to his place before. "Take me home."

TWENTY-FOUR

T HE NEXT EVENING, BACK AT home, my hands held my Baileys Irish Cream like a lifeline as the waves pounded relentlessly against the shore past the edge of my property line. A storm was coming, and I didn't mean the one that was rolling across the horizon, soon to hit our area. I was more concerned about the one unfurling at work as well as at home, which seemed to be moving all the people in my life around like life-sized chess pieces.

"You need anything?" Trev called from the kitchen.

I mumbled that I did not, my gaze never leaving the horizon, my hand frozen with the drink halfway to my lips. I was still upset about our argument about the sweater the day before. Something was wrong. No matter how much I wanted to, I couldn't ignore the warning my mom had given me about the letter: "*Think of this as a sort of Pandora's box, or Pandora's letter, if you will. Only open it—and I mean only—if strange and unexplainable things are happening. And especially if you feel you are in danger.*"

The sweater was just one example.

I would open it soon, but I wanted a few more hours of

denial and of normalcy before I faced whatever was inside that letter. I could do without unleashing Pandora's horrors.

Not only did I want time, but I also preferred to avoid the headache that gripped my skull when I even thought about opening the envelope. The closer I was to doing it, the stronger the pain became, as if my mind was trying to warn me away. Whatever secret was inside, there'd been a reason why my mom had wanted me to live a life without its burden. I knew I wouldn't have that luxury much longer.

The clank of dishes paused, as Trev must have finished loading the dishwasher from the meal I'd prepared. He'd wanted to order in or cook for me, but he didn't understand how preparing food soothed my soul.

When he volunteered to clean up, as he often did, I jumped on his offer. I needed to sit and process. I'd already done that enough, and the letter would be there later that night or the next day. It wasn't going anywhere, and I still wasn't ready to face its secrets. I wanted a few more hours with him, pretending my life wasn't one big disaster after another.

Trev took the seat across from me at my small kitchen table overlooking the beach. I offered him a small smile, determined to push my worries aside for the next couple of hours. "Did Carl give you any trouble after I dropped you off this morning?"

During our argument the night before, he'd sworn we were there together after we'd gone on his boat. It wasn't true. I don't know what was going on, but one way or another, I would figure it out. Carl hadn't been a problem that day. "Carl wasn't at work."

"Is that unusual?"

I knew Trev was trying to do his job and make sure everyone was where he or she was supposed to be and wasn't a suspect or trying to hurt me. It wasn't Carl. "He probably went ahead and left for Washington early. I know he had a meeting that I wasn't scheduled to attend."

Trev took a sip of his drink before setting it on the table. He knocked his knuckles against the wood surface before standing. "Why don't we get out of here and go for a walk on the beach?"

"No. I'd rather not." I grabbed his empty cup and took it to the sink. I had a sip or two left in mine. With a glance over my shoulder, I went into the living room. Trev followed.

The water looked rough, but that wasn't the reason for my refusal. I wanted to feel his arms around me again. Even though we'd argued, I trusted him. It had been a rough week, and… I didn't know. I wanted to believe he could've thought I'd been to his place when he'd merely brought my sweater in from the car and forgotten he had. We were both focused on bigger things. Maybe I truly was losing my mind, but I didn't care at the moment. All I wanted was to feel alive—with him.

I tossed him the remote, and he settled on the couch. I turned toward the kitchen to put my mug away before joining him in front of the TV.

He draped his arm around my shoulders, and when he turned to me, I let the desire that was slowly burning at all times when he was around flame to its fullest and show in my expression. Butterflies erupted in my stomach as the remote fell from his hand. His eyes dilated, and he drew me close.

The accelerated beat of my heart echoed in my ears, and a hot flush crept up my face as he cupped my cheek. I alternated from his expressive eyes to his lips as he dipped his head down. My eyelids fluttered closed at the first brush of his lips against mine. With soft strokes, he traced my lower lip then the seam of my mouth until I opened for him. His tongue teased mine, exploring and deepening the kiss. Needing to be closer, I arched my back, wanting to crawl into his skin.

With ease, he lifted me until I was sitting astride him, his lips never leaving mine. His fingers threaded through the back of my hair, cradling my head. He tightened his grip, tilting the angle of my head. A gasp left me as he tore his mouth from mine only to trail kisses from the corner of my mouth, along my jawline, and finally to my neck.

I ran my fingers through his hair, loosening it so it fell from the bun he'd haphazardly fashioned earlier in loose waves. A moan filled the minuscule space between us, and I belatedly realized it had come from me. As he bit between my shoulder and neck, sending a sharp spike of desire through me, I ground my hips against his hard length.

In one smooth motion, he stood, and I wrapped my legs tightly around his waist. My head fell back as he continued his exploration of my neck and the tops of my breasts. Vaguely, I was aware that he was walking us toward my bedroom. We bumped into the doorframe, and he mumbled something, but I didn't care. I wanted more of him.

He lowered me to my bed, and I sucked in a breath at the sexy image he presented. His blond waves fell around his sinfully handsome face, and his strong jaw coupled with sharp cheekbones and hungry eyes sent another wave of desire through me. He reached behind his head, gripped his T-shirt, and yanked it off. I lost myself in the flexing of his muscles as he moved. His abs tightened as he pushed his hair away from his face. I followed the path of his hands as he undid his belt and jeans. The deep rumble of his voice tore me from the sight of his clothes leaving his body. I blinked, trying to understand what he was asking me.

"Is this okay? Are you sure you want to do this?"

I nodded, not able to summon my voice, my mind a swirling haze of need.

"Jules"—amusement colored his face in a wicked half grin —"I need to hear you say you want this too."

"Yes." I barely recognized my voice. It was husky, infused with want. "I'm sure."

That got me what I wanted. He tugged my jeans off, and I helped with my shirt and bra. He tore my panties off, almost causing me to combust before he even did anything.

"You're so beautiful."

I reached for him, desperate to feel his heavy weight over me.

"Let me look at you."

He bent one of my legs then pulled me toward the edge of the bed. He dropped to his knees, and I gasped at the press of his tongue between my legs as he licked and tasted me. As he laved, circling the pulsating bundle of nerves at my center, a primitive desire eclipsed all but what he was doing—or not doing. I felt him slide one finger inside, then two, and as he sucked on my clit, I exploded, my body tightening and my back arching. Stars burst behind my lids.

I heard the crinkle of a condom wrapper. After another second, he covered my body with his. I grabbed a fistful of his hair as my mouth found his demanding lips. He spread my legs wide, cradling my head with one hand, my lower back with the other. Lust built inside of me, tightening my abdomen, making me slick for him. I ground my hips against his. He lifted me. I felt weightless, a puppet to his needs. I wrapped my legs around his waist.

On his knees on the mattress, he held me suspended, teasing my entrance until I blinked my desire-clouded eyes at him. My heart pounded at the connection between us. We both moaned as he entered, filling me, hard and fast. I pushed against him. He changed the angle, and my head fell back, my body pulsing around him. A scream tore from my throat as I came again. Growling, he increased the pace then followed as we both hurdled over the edge. He dropped his face to my neck as we caught our breath.

I whimpered as he pulled out, and he cradled me against him for a few seconds before he discarded the condom. Back in his arms, our heartbeats slowed, and I lay beside him in contentment, feeling satisfied and full for the first time in a very long time. I drifted in and out of sleep, waking when he ran his fingers along my arm.

The fan turned in a lazy circle overhead as thunder rumbled outside. I cuddled closer to Trev, my head resting on his chest and our legs tangled together. His hand traced absent circles on my shoulder, and I sighed. *If only life could be so uncomplicated and perfect all the time.* I splayed my palm across his washboard stomach, about to suggest round two when he tensed beneath me.

"Do you smell that?"

I inhaled and jackknifed into a sitting position. Before I could get out of bed, Trev launched himself up and threw on his jeans. Barefoot, he raced from the room. I tore the sheet from the bed and wrapped it around my body as best as I could while racing to follow him.

I skidded to a halt as he was turning the oven's knobs back to their upright, off position.

"Open the windows," he ordered as he bent over the lit candle on the counter.

With one puff, he blew it out, and I held my breath, praying the gas leaking from the stove didn't cause us to die in an explosion.

I raced to the slider that led off the kitchen to the back of the house, flipped the lock, and yanked it all the way open as he did the same with the window above the sink. Lightning split the sky. Three seconds later, thunder boomed like a bad omen.

He closed the distance between us, his features set in fierce lines, and I shivered at the intensity. Before I knew it, he'd bent and scooped me up against his bare chest. He carried me outside and several feet from the house. His hands gripped me tightly against him, and by the way he held me, I didn't think he would let me go. Clutching the sheet in one hand, I snaked my other one around his neck.

An equally fierce looking man appeared from the tree line. I tensed until Connor's features registered—I'd met him. Two more men appeared from different areas around my house. I didn't know them. *God, I wish I was dressed.*

Connor made some hand gesture, and the other two went inside my house.

Trev explained what had happened and why we were outside. After a while, Connor and the other two gave the okay to go back inside. The men I didn't know were eyeing me strangely, with suspicion. I didn't like it.

"I didn't light that candle." My defensive reaction kicked in.

"Who was in the kitchen last?" Connor asked.

It didn't look good. "I was." I had to admit it, but I swung my gaze to Trev's. "I didn't light it. I know I didn't."

He squeezed me against him. "I believe you."

All tension fell from my muscles at the sincerity of his words. Connor's lifted eyebrow told me he was skeptical, but I was only worried about what Trev thought.

"The house should be clear. We turned on the fans."

At Connor's confirmation that the house was sufficiently aired out, we went back in. I needed to get dressed. Once inside, Trev lowered me to my feet. He stood in the kitchen with a furrowed brow.

"I'm going to put some clothes on."

He nodded absently, and I went to my bedroom, cleaned up, and threw on the clothes from earlier. As I dressed, I ran over everything that'd happened. Everything pointed to me, from the message on my monitor and mirror, falling overboard, Fran's identical wound and death, the candles, things being moved around, and finally to the gas leaks. I looked guilty, even if it wasn't true.

TWENTY-FIVE

"Are you sure you want me here for this?" Trev's thigh pressed against mine on the couch. I leaned against him so that he, too, could read what I was about to—the letter from my mom.

We were both fully clothed. I'd made coffee, and our cups sat on the table, untouched. "I'm sure."

My fingers trembled as they traced my name, Juliana, written in my mom's flowing script. It was time to open the letter. I no longer had the luxury of pretending that the things that were happening were just coincidence, unfortunate occurrences, or tragedies that didn't have anything to do with me. They did. In one way or another, I was the center of the storm.

Dear Juliana,

I'm so very proud of you. You're my whole world. Not only are you smart—I'd say a genius—but you're humble, kind, compassionate, and so very beautiful, both inside and out. Some of my favorite memories are of the times you and I have spent cooking together. It warms my heart that we were able to carry on the traditions passed down through all the women in our family. My mother and grand-mother would be so proud of you. In fact, I know they are.

Hold on to my love and the conviction of how much you mean to both myself and your father. He loved you more than you'll ever know. I have to believe that in your heart, you feel his devotion to you. We would do anything to keep you safe, to have you grow up as the stunning woman you have become.

Here is the part I dread sharing. It's been a blessing that you have no memories from before the accident, and if you are reading this letter, I'm afraid your life has turned upside down in ways you cannot explain. With or without your memories of when we lived in Italy, I want to share with you why your father and I decided to do what we did.

I'm going to begin with the part of your past that is suppressed. While the accident was the catalyst for your amnesia, I believe your mind continued to shield you from what had happened as self-preservation. It must be time for you to remember, if no other reason than preserving your safety.

You're an identical twin.

You were born three minutes after your sister. As toddlers, there were issues that we wrote off as normal sibling behavior, until it became apparent that your sister would do things that warranted closer scru-tiny. Anabella couldn't stand you getting any attention from either your father or me, especially your father. Because of that, we were careful to have any praise be equal and doled out at the same time. Not only that, but gifts had to be identical and given together. That helped for many years, but not nearly enough, as she destroyed anything you were given.

Of course, we had your sister in therapy. The problem was, she is equally as bright, even though your fields are different. She is not one to underestimate. I love Anabella, but I am not blind to her faults. As you both grew, more and more accidents would happen that you would be the victim of. Many times, we could not prove your sister was at fault. You did trip and bump into things a lot as it was. My darling, I say this with love, but you are not the most graceful. Even as an adult, you have all sorts of mysterious bruises from when your head is in the clouds figuring out some problem or other. That wasn't a concern. What was alarming was when Bella took things too far. The cuts on your arm were not self-inflicted.

Your father and I will never forgive ourselves for the things that happened to you. There were times when Bella stayed in mental institutions. They never stuck. She fooled everyone, all the doctors, and there was no way we could convince them otherwise. But we knew.

It wasn't until shortly before we vacationed from our home in Italy and traveled through Europe to visit family that your father and I came up with a way for you both to have fulfilling and safe lives. We planned to part ways, each taking one of our daughters to raise. There would be no contact between the two of you.

The day we were out on the boat and the storm hit, we knew it would be our chance. We'd been keeping a close eye on Bella. She'd get this mischievous look that almost always led to trouble for you. The accident that day was fate. We'd never thought two boats colliding would allow us to save you like it had.

You went over, not from the other boat hitting ours, but because of your sister. That happened almost immediately after the boats crashed. When Bella shoved you overboard, your father grabbed her and held her against his chest. That's when I jumped over the rail and went after you. Your head injury was from debris that fell into the water, knocking you unconscious. I was able to get to you and keep you afloat until help arrived.

Your father kept Bella from seeing me go over.

My sweet Juliana, your sister is alive. If anything happens that you cannot explain, it's her. If accidents happen that people think are your fault, but you know for a fact are not, know that it's your sister. Get help immediately. Bella must have found out where you are and that you did not die that day in the water. It pains me to say this, but she believed there should have been only one of you, that you were a genetic mutation. A mistake. A clone of herself that carried only weak elements but also stole what was rightfully hers.

She's sick, Juliana.

Not knowing of your existence enabled her to live a normal life, but I fear that after your father passed of a heart attack last year (I'm so sorry you weren't able to grow up with him in your life), she may one day find evidence that we are alive. Your father and I tried to be so careful, but secrets have a way of coming out. We'd hoped this one never would.

I love you more than anything. Please be safe. Hire guards. Do everything you can to protect yourself. This time, when Bella comes for you, she will be determined to finish the job she attempted twice before—ending your life.

Be safe, my beautiful daughter,
Mom

The letter dropped from my hands, and bile climbed in my throat. My mouth filled with saliva. *I'm going to be sick.* I pushed away from Trev and ran to the bathroom, where I fell to my knees. I emptied my stomach while my head splintered with resurfacing memories from the newly open door in my mind.

God, Bella. I remember you. I suddenly remembered *everything.* Sobs wracked my body. Nothing would ever be okay again. Black spots bled the edges of my vision that would soon take over, leaving me unconscious after the shock of processing so much. I knew without a shadow of a doubt that she was coming for me.

CLOUDS BLANKETED THE SKY, BLOCKING the sun's warm rays. The morning matched my mood. I understood why my mom had withheld the information about my sister—she'd wanted me to have a normal life. But knowledge was power. I should have disregarded her wishes and opened that letter a long time ago.

There was no point in dwelling on what I should have done. Instead, I would focus on the best way to stay safe. After stirring in creamer, I took a fortifying sip of coffee then met Trev's gaze across the table.

After I'd passed out, he'd held me. We'd both read the letter, and he'd understood the toll it'd taken. The rest of the night, I'd spent alternating with sobbing in his arms and fitful, restless sleep. When morning finally came, I was ready to face it.

Remorse and worry darkened Trev's blue eyes. "None of us gave a second thought to finding out anything about your dad and sister. Since you said they died in Italy, it was a moot point, but one we shouldn't have disregarded."

"It's not your fault." I pursed my lips.

Reading my mom's words had brought everything back. She hadn't been kidding—what she'd written had been a virtual Pandora's box. Maybe "key" was a better way of describing the contents, as they'd unlocked the door to every hidden memory that'd shielded me from my past.

I recalled the time Bella had sliced open my arm in the bathroom. The mirror scare I'd had recently, where I'd thought the person staring back at me hadn't been my face, was true— I'd seen my sister's face superimposed over mine while memories leaked out. Only at the time, I couldn't make sense of them.

Suddenly, I could.

She'd been so angry, and I'd been terrified. We were in the bathroom, and her fingers dug deep into the base of my hand as she held the kitchen knife. A dark gleam shimmered over her eyes as she growled, "You're always in the way, taking what's mine."

I'd cried out as she brandished the weapon. At the first dip of the blade, blood spurted from my severed skin, and I sank to the ground while she continued slicing.

With a shake of my head, I forced the gruesome memory to fade. I understood why my mom hadn't wanted me to remember, as there was so much that wasn't pretty, even more than she and dad had known about.

"You wouldn't have found much," I said. "When my mom and I came to America, we did so under her maiden name. We had new identities."

"Bella has your father's last name?"

"I'd assume so. It was DeLuca."

Trev stood and pulled his cell phone from his pocket. He paced the kitchen. "Chris. Run a check and facial-recognition locator for Anabella DeLuca, Jules's twin sister."

I tuned out the rest of his conversation, preoccupied by remembering a life where my family had been whole, or as much as it could have been. I'd loved my sister. She'd hurt me.

At the time, she was my world, aside from my parents—she was my identical twin.

I vaguely recognized Trev approach, off his cell, before another ping came through. He would be able to find Bella with the facial-location software by ruling out where I was. Maybe we could put the nightmare behind us before someone else was hurt.

But I hadn't been the only target. I gasped as all the air left my lungs. *Fran.* The way she died suddenly made sense, as did the time freezing on my clock. Horror filled me at the realization of what Bella had done and what she was capable of. We had to stop her.

"Are you expecting someone?" Trev disconnected the call then tapped out a text.

I shook my head.

Pounding at the door mirrored the jackhammers going to town in my head. I stood to answer it, but Trev stepped in front of me, shielding me from whoever was there.

Blue and red lights flashed as he opened the door, his right hand obscured from the view from outside, at his side with his gun drawn and pointed at the floor. "Can I help you?"

My heart thudded in my chest, and I placed my palm flat against his back. I needed his strength. It had to be about Fran. I rested my forehead against his tense muscles, just above my hand. An ominous wave washed over me as I heard the officer ask if I was home. *This won't end well.*

"I am," I spoke from behind Trev before he could incriminate himself trying to protect me. And he would've—I could feel it in the way his body went from tense to rock hard.

Taking a deep breath, I stepped to the side and faced my fate.

"Dr. Juliana Moretti."

My shoulders went back, and I tilted my chin up. "Yes."

"You're under arrest for the attempted murder of Carl Alderidge."

"What?" *Carl? My mind went numb.*

They read me my rights. As I was getting in the squad car, Trev assured me that he'd get me out right away, and then we were pulling out in a blaze of flashing red and blue.

A tear tracked down my cheek. *Bella.* I closed my eyes, remembering all the nights we'd lie in bed across from one another, back before she'd changed and we shared a room… Before she hated me. The shift came more often as she shied away from her version of our shared name, Ana, taken from Juliana and Anabella. My thoughts sifted through memories until one burst into clarity.

"Ana." Anabella stretched her hand across the space between our twin beds. "Matt pushed me on the swings."

I grinned and clasped her hand in mine. "Are you gonna marry him?"

"Maybe. But if I do, you have to marry his brother."

"Ew. I'm not marrying Louis, Ana." I scrunched my nose. "Yuck. He's mean."

"You have to. We're the same. We can't be apart."

"Then you marry Louis. He doesn't try to trip you." I hated Matt's brother.

Anabella refused to listen to me. She always wanted her way. "That's not how it works." Her eyes narrowed, and I cried out as she dug her fingers into mine. "Tomorrow, we'll play tag with them."

The scary shift in the way she spoke sent chills up my arm. I didn't like it when she talked to me like that. I jerked my hand back and rolled over. "I'm tired," I said. "Night, Ana."

I bit my lip and waited, wondering if she would be mad. She'd been getting angry with me lately, and I didn't know why. I missed my sister. She'd wanted to use our shared name less and less. Sometimes she was Bella and I was Jules, instead of both of us using Ana. I didn't want her to go away.

"Night," Anabella mumbled, and I let my eyes drift shut.

"Ma'am."

I jolted from the memory while the officer hovered over me. Bella and I had been six years old, and things hadn't become horrible yet, but they were getting there. Bella, no longer Ana to the rest of the world, began to use our shared name to get me in trouble, pretending she was me.

The officer stood outside the open car door. "Please get out."

Chaos swirled in my head, testing then rejecting possible variables behind what my sister would gain from impersonating me. My legs buckled, and the officer held me up. *Could this be her kindest way yet of getting me out of the way? Locking me away from the world, rather than ending my life?*

TREV

WHEN I'D LEANED OVER THE squad car door before the officer shut it, it had taken everything in me to stay calm. Jules was on her way to the police station, and the fact that I hadn't been able to prevent her from going there in the first place ate at my conscience. We should have caught the issue with her sister. Instead, we'd focused on the man who'd attacked her twice, not a hidden threat within her family.

I'd have her out in a few hours, tops. *Fuck. I can't believe this happened.* First things first, I needed to contact Rich while coordinating with my team—thankfully, Mike was available when I sent him a text telling him to get the lawyers on it immediately.

I ground my teeth as the phone rang once, twice, three times. *Pick up, dammit.*

"Rich Stevens."

I skipped the greeting. He had caller ID. "I need your help."

"You'll have to give me more to go on, Trev." Papers shuffled on his end, then a door closed.

"The woman you volunteered me to guard."

"Carl Alderidge's scientist, Dr. Moretti? What about her?"

"She was arrested a few minutes ago for allegedly putting Carl in the hospital. We have an alibi, but not one that will hold up against attempted murder or against the charges that are sure to follow regarding the death of her former assistant, Fran Jones."

"Carl is injured?"

"He's at the hospital and in a medically induced coma. They haven't been able to get any information from him yet. The evidence we have is from the doorman, who confirms that the picture of Jules matches the woman who was last seen visiting Carl. He was unconscious when he was found by his cleaning lady earlier this morning."

"Why did the police suspect Jules enough to show a picture of her to the doorman?"

"Some colleagues of Jules confirmed that they'd gotten in a disagreement, and it was enough for them to be suspicious, I guess." The whole thing had become a giant headache.

"What do you need from me?" Carl asked.

I filled him in about Anabella and how we'd messed up by not doing a full-scale background check and finding out about her. I pinched the bridge of my nose. The job had seemed like a cut-and-dried babysitting gig at first. I wanted to punch something.

With a push of a button, I switched to speaker then forwarded the picture I'd taken on my phone of Jules's mom's letter. My cell was pinging like crazy while I talked to Rich, and pounding resumed on the front door. I let Connor in, waved him to the table, and continued my conversation. "They're going to take their time at the station. I wasn't able to get them to release what they have on Jules to hold her."

"What have you done so far?" The click of a door sounded, and Rich asked his assistant to get the police chief on the phone.

"I texted Mike to get the lawyers over there so we can find

out what they have on Jules. I have a feeling it's DNA evidence, but that shouldn't hold her there, as we're bringing new information that they won't have about identical twins to their attention."

"You want a mouth swab test done?" Rich guessed.

"God, yes." That one only took a few hours and could determine the DNA differences between twins. "The other method would take too long." The standard one was expensive and required sequencing of the entire genome. Subtle or rare variations took a month to analyze, and we didn't have that luxury. The swab test used a chemical that would target DNA points—differences between twins could easily be determined that way. "I need you to use your connections to make that happen. You should have grounds to expedite, as she was due to fly to Washington DC today to administer the next batch of injections to your military program."

"I agree. That'll help cut through red tape, especially when she was going to use a new vector. Carl being in the hospital puts us at a severe disadvantage."

I couldn't even think beyond using any advantage we had at our disposal. I didn't care if he was listing off gains for him rather than concern for Jules. I wanted her out of there.

When she was released, I would be able to protect her, and I wouldn't leave her side. In there, she had to be scared and stressed. I hated that I couldn't get to her—although Anabella couldn't, either.

TWENTY-SEVEN

I CLASPED JULES'S HAND IN mine as we exited the police station. I slipped my thumb under the cuff of her shirt and caressed the base of her scar. I wasn't sure which one of us I comforted by anchoring us by touch—maybe both of us.

Rich and our team of lawyers had come through, and Jules had held firm during questioning, stating she'd never set foot in Carl's lakefront penthouse. Several hours later, the swab test revealed that what she'd said was true. She hadn't been the one at Carl's home. And with that, they had no reason to hold her.

"What about Fran?" Tension clung to Jules's question.

I squeezed her palm, ushering her into my vehicle. Rounding the side, I got in and pulled into traffic before answering. "They'll reopen her case. The incision that matches the one on your arm and what your mom said in the letter is proof enough to cast doubt on your sister."

"They'll find traces of Bella there. It destroys me that Fran was murdered—but knowing that if she woke, she would have thought it was me? God, I…"

"She had to have known something didn't add up. You would never have hurt her."

"I hope so."

As she turned to stare out her window, I clenched my teeth, counting silently to ease my spiked blood pressure. I wanted to fix it for her and to make everyone who'd hurt her suffer. Minutes ticked by until Jules faced me once more.

"That day you said we were on a boat during work hours"—her face contorted in a grimace—"it wasn't me. You took Bella out."

Goddamn. Bile rose in the back of my throat. She hadn't been acting like herself. Thank God I didn't sleep with her sister. I told Jules as much.

"It wouldn't have mattered." Her sad eyes met mine. "I wouldn't have held you responsible. My sister… She thinks I'm a mistake and that I shouldn't have been born. She wants everything that's mine, and she'll take or destroy whatever she has to have it. I can't guess her motivation, aside from the disillusioned thought that whatever I have is meant to be hers. But I'm so grateful she didn't hurt you."

"The more I think about that day, the more I remember how often I thought your—well, her—behavior wasn't consistent with what I knew of you." I turned onto her street, and silence fell between us. Her exhaustion was palpable. I needed to get her safely inside her home.

My phone buzzed. After parking, I pulled it out. Connor would arrive in an hour. He had information from Chris, and apparently, it was something I needed to see.

JULES

MY HANDS CURLED AROUND THE mug of coffee Trev handed me. The heady scent of cinnamon and cream helped to soothe my dragging spirit. The warmth of the mug further relaxed me, and I sank into the couch next to him. It was late in the afternoon and not long after we'd left the police station. There was no way I could even think of work. The rest of my time today would be spent at home, with Trev.

"She wasn't always like this." Thoughts of my sister played on repeat.

"Anabella?" The TV was on with the volume low. I soaked up the strength and heat from his body, lying my head against his chest.

I nodded. "We used to fight when we were little. But we were also friends, for the most part." I thought about that some more. "Well, so long as I did what she wanted." He swept my legs onto his lap, and I let out a sigh of contentment.

"And your parents? Did they treat you the same or defer to her moods?"

I let his question marinate for a few seconds. "A combination, I think. They tried to curb her temper, but then it seemed they just removed either her or me from whatever the issue was. As we got older, Bella wanted independence. When I tagged along with her, it was okay until it wasn't."

"How did she handle you being around when she wanted to do her own thing?"

I liked that he was letting me talk. I wanted to work out my feelings for my twin. Feeling as if I was half of a person without her sucked. When I didn't remember my past, I had a sense of loss, but my life was fulfilling. With Bella in the same city, I wanted to maintain my individuality. She wasn't good for me, even if she was a part of me. "My family dealt with her as best they could. Bella connected with my dad more, as she was adventurous. I liked to hang out in the kitchen with my mom." I shrugged. "It worked well enough."

Trev ran his fingers through my hair in long, dragging strokes.

"At least until about the time we realized boys were… carriers of cooties."

His chest vibrated as deep laughter spilled forth. "Ah, the era of cooties."

I smiled. "Yeah. Then we both had our first crush, and I became a whole new level of competition to my sister. It was then that she told me I shouldn't exist and that since nature hadn't corrected its mistake, she would do so."

My sister was a twisted being.

TWENTY-EIGHT

DARKNESS HAD FALLEN, AND THE air had turned a few degrees cooler. Jules was dozing on the couch. I hadn't planned for her to miss out on the meeting with Connor, but she needed to rest. From the cover of the trees, a dark form separated from the inky void to my left. I recognized Connor's shape as he came closer. When he lifted his hand, I caught sight of a folder. We would need light, so I motioned for him to follow me inside.

The sliding-glass door rolled with a soft rumble as we stepped over the threshold. "Beer, water?"

I went to the counter to get a glass of some water for myself and, at his nod, one for him too.

"The men we have watching the house are aware of her twin." Connor accepted the cup then took a seat at the table. The folder slapped against the surface.

I sat down and flipped the file open as Connor talked.

"Chris and Jack found a connection between the two villagers and the scientist, Sasha Orlova."

"The one who died? And the family she stayed with?"

"Yes," Connor confirmed. "In Siberia. Their family's nephew is an archeologist who was engaged to Sasha."

I lifted a picture of Omar Romanov, who was five feet, eleven inches tall, with dark, almost black hair. He had broad shoulders on a wiry frame. "Where is he working?"

"He was on a dig until a day after the Russian scientist died. The site hasn't heard from him since."

Sasha. So the link for at least some of the issues surrounding Jules was due to the unknown hemorrhagic fever outbreak in Russia, but I wasn't following why. "Is Omar's connection with Sasha or with the family she stayed with who died?"

Connor crossed his arms behind his head and tipped the chair to balance precariously on its back legs. "Yuri and Tiana Romanov were his aunt and uncle. Sasha was his fiancé."

Revenge. "So Omar targeted the laboratory and specifically Jules once he learned she developed the formula the Russian scientists were using. Going out on a limb here and guessing he's angry because his fiancée and family didn't benefit from Jules's help, even though her formula could have potentially saved them."

"Seems that way."

"What we haven't figured out yet is how he gained knowledge about the restricted vector." I rubbed my hand over my tired eyes. "The antibody shot, sure—that's what Jules was sharing with Russia. But the gene-editing tool kit, she'd have to get permission for." Omar had to be connected in some way, and how high up would be the determining factor. We had to know if he planned to use it for his country while they launched biowarfare.

"Rich is aware of the threat, and we have all eyes out for Omar and permission to question him, should we find him first." Connor's fist clenched. "We need to assume the worst."

"We do." I couldn't have agreed more. "Do we have any idea where he is?" I committed the picture of Omar's wide forehead, deep-set dark eyes, oddly proportioned frame, and square jaw to memory. In contrast to Jules's five-five and slight build, he would've appeared much taller. My focus strayed to Jules as I assured myself she that was on the couch, resting and safe.

"Chris is working on facial recognition to see if he pops up anywhere. I'm sure Rich has other people on it too."

"Because of the nature of the deaths and who was involved, I wonder if Omar fed the head of the Russian lab information about the restricted military vector."

"Makes sense." Connor dropped his chair back to its rightful position. "But how did Omar learn about it in the first place?"

"That is the question, isn't it?"

A TRICKLE OF SUNLIGHT SPLASHED across the bed, tiptoeing over Jules's sheet-covered hip. My arms tightened around her, and she cuddled closer, a sigh escaping her parted lips. The fan of her long, thick eyelashes cast a spiky web over her high cheekbones.

If only we could stay in bed all day today, but we can't.

I had to find Omar and question him, and Jules insisted that she had to go in to the office. Once past the front desk, she would be safe. They'd been alerted about the sister, and Jules had a restricted-security-clearance-access card and a finger-print scan that let the staff know she was the twin who was allowed inside.

I glanced at the clock. We had about two minutes before the alarm was going to go off. I wanted to savor the moments with her in my arms. Fear had a choke hold on her—on me— but I had to believe that she would be safe. Part of the worry came from not being able to be at her side twenty-four seven, though I knew the police were looking for both Omar and

Bella due to the attack on Carl. After we caught Omar, I would override Jules's protests about job shadowing. She would be okay during work hours, and I would find him.

Jules stirred again, and I groaned. *If only we had time before she had to go to the office, we could make love again.* I knew her internal alarm was going off, though the actual one had one more minute. I pressed my lips to her forehead, and her lashes fluttered open. Sleep-drugged eyes blinked at me. Unable to resist, I dropped to her soft, plump lips, brushing mine over them. She wiggled impossibly closer as I tugged her bottom lip into my mouth.

The shrill beep of her alarm went off, and we pulled apart, both of us grinning. "Guess that's our cue, huh?" I would haven given anything to stay there with her, but we both had time constraints. "Tonight, you're all mine."

A delicate flush infused her cheeks, and I gave in to one more long, exploratory kiss. She felt so right in my arms. How I got so lucky to have found her was beyond me.

Reluctantly, we pulled apart. While she jumped into the shower, I went to the kitchen to make coffee. If I'd followed her, we would have been an hour late to work, but she'd told me how much she wanted to finish the testing for the healing salve so it could be sent off for FDA approval. Given the military connection for the product, the tool kit's vector, and the antibody injections, the FDA time had been fast-tracked.

I understood why it was so important to her and didn't even try to argue. The scar on her arm caused her a lot of distress. If she'd had the salve when the injury occurred, there would've been a good chance that the scar would have been minimal. Plastic surgery was another option she'd been considering, but she had rejected the idea of it. I would support her decision either way. The mark didn't bother me from an aesthetic angle, though the meaning behind it did.

I felt her approach. Her arms wrapped around my waist, and she pressed against my back.

"Your turn." Jules leaned around me and smiled. "I'll make breakfast."

"Coffee's on the counter."

"Mm, thank you."

She was such a coffee fiend. Before I'd finished pointing to where I'd set her mug, she had it in her hands. That was my cue to shower. We had twenty minutes to finish getting ready, eat, and be out the door.

A shrill ring sounded from Jules's phone. While cooking, she lifted the phone to her ear. "It's Becs." She let me know before focusing on the call. Silence stretched as I listened to Jules try unsuccessfully to get a word in. A full minute passed before she did.

"I'm okay. I swear." She flashed me a panicked look. "We should use a code word. That way you'll know it's me. Wait a sec." She handed the phone to me and then brandished her scarred arm. "Tell her you have proof it's me before I tell her the code word."

"Becs." I growled in the phone. "What's going on?" I needed in on what was happening.

Her friend's frantic voice pierced my eardrum. "I got a call from a blocked number, and I answered it, you know, because of all the crazy things happening and I was worried about Jules. This person said she was Jules and that I needed to come to her right away. That she was scared. I said I would then hung up and called Jules's cell to make sure it was her. It wasn't! Please tell me you're doing something to keep her safe. From what Jules told me, her sister is dangerous."

I assured Becs we would keep Jules safe and cautioned her about accepting any calls unless Jules said the code word they'd come up with. Bella was getting desperate. I would get my hands on her soon.

It took another few minutes for Jules to get off the phone with her friend and to calm down. Knowing that Becs wouldn't come to us was reassuring. Bella couldn't be in two places at once, and it seemed that Jules was highest on her priority list.

Breakfast passed quickly, and after we'd cleaned up the dishes, we headed to her research facility. Not much later, I pulled up in front of her office building. I'd shown her the picture of Omar and explained what we thought and what to do if she spotted him on our drive.

Jules leaned over, and the scent of magnolias wrapped around me as she pressed a kiss to my mouth.

"Be safe." I wanted to follow her, but my phone pinged with a text. The fact she would be surrounded by tightened security in the building aided in my letting her go inside without me.

As she shifted away with her hand on the door handle, she flashed me a confident grin. "I will. I'll text you before I head down at the end of the day. Probably about five. I think I can get everything finished early."

Throwing the car in Park illegally, I got out and rounded to her side because I would feel better if I walked her inside. She threaded our fingers together as we matched our pace to the door. I scanned the area. A sixth sense prickled my awareness. He was nearby.

I spared a glance at my phone. It was Chris: *Omar sighted a few blocks from Jules's building.* At the large glass door, I squeezed her hand once before she released me and made her way to security. Not until she passed through and waved did I turn. From the corner of my eye, I caught a flash of a man who fit Omar's description leaning against the outside edge of the building and facing away. My gut said it was him.

I sprinted to the end of the building. The sidewalk was crowded, but not enough to hinder my path. When I was an arm's length away, he turned. *Got him.*

THE SMELL OF BLEACH CLUNG to the open storage unit we'd converted some time ago into an interrogation room. We'd combined two side-by-side cells so that one held a small, segregated office, and the main one could fit an SUV and had a drainage pipe for easy wash down after questioning. It'd been a while since we'd used the space—the last time was because of Hawk and Stella, but I couldn't let my mind wander there. I needed answers.

Connor stood next to me with his arms crossed over his chest. Omar was zip-tied to a steel chair bolted into the ground. One punch to the jaw around the side of Jules's office building, and he'd gone down. From there, I'd hoisted him over my shoulder, shoved him into the back of the SUV, and contacted Connor to meet me.

I took point, but Connor's intimidating presence served a necessary purpose. I wanted Omar off-balance. Silence stretched as I contemplated what I wanted to do. Violence bled from my pores, but that wasn't how I wanted to conduct his questioning, at least not entirely. After a few well-placed hits and threats, Omar's agitation, discomfort, and fear were at a fine point where he would talk.

Omar strained against his restraints. "Holding me won't stop anything."

Interesting. "How's that?"

Connor moved around behind Omar and pressed a gun to his temple. We wouldn't pull the trigger, but he didn't know that. The clock was ticking on whatever would happen to Jules. I could feel it in my bones.

Beads of sweat formed on Omar's forehead and above his lip. I shifted my gaze from him to Connor. Omar broke. "Anabella."

Goddamn it. "How do you know her?"

"I met her first. Thought she was the scientist. I went after her, but she explained who she was, and I saw Juliana then too. We're working together."

"Why did you go after Jules in the first place? She didn't have anything to do with Sasha or your aunt and uncle."

"She could have helped them!"

It would go nowhere. He was acting out of grief, and I doubted he would listen, but I had to set the record straight. "No one knew they'd contracted the illness. When Sasha's boss reached out to Jules's employer, it was too late."

Deranged laughter spilled from Omar's lips. "She'll pay. A life for a life."

TWENTY-
NINE

AFTER GOING THROUGH LOBBY SECURITY, I slowed my pace. Only a few minutes had passed since Trev had dropped me at work, but I didn't have it in me to rush upstairs—I suddenly missed Fran with a vengeance. I was tired and dragging. The sublime scent of coffee drew my gaze to the little café tucked near the elevators. There wasn't enough caffeine in the world to get me through the day, and the thought of having a latte, as opposed to a subpar drink from the coffee machine we had in our break room, was too great to pass up. I was stopping there first.

Another wave of sadness crashed over me as I stepped into the small café, but the scent of coffee beans and sugar hit me like a balm, and I moved to the counter, a little more balanced in my loneliness. I wouldn't ever forget Fran, but I was finding my way again, especially with Becs's and Trev's unwavering support.

The barista was in a mad dash, filling an order that had probably been called in ahead of time from upstairs. She finished fitting four cups into a cardboard tray before she cast a hurried glance my way. "What'll it be?"

I placed my order while her phone rang nonstop. It wasn't busy inside, but the barista was a flurry of motion, trying to keep up with the phone orders.

I dropped into a chair in the rear corner and flipped through my email on my phone while I waited. My thoughts turned back to Becs. I was relieved she lived a good distance away. If I let myself dwell on the what-ifs of her residing nearby while Bella was stalking those around me, terror would have had a firm choke hold on me. For the time being, I thought she was safe—not only that, but she was aware of my twin, which Fran and Carl hadn't been.

"Here you are."

I looked up and flashed a small smile at the harried barista, who'd delivered my cinnamon-and-cream latte with barely a glance before dashing back to her orders. I took a sip, and my eyelids drifted closed. *Heaven. Seriously, I needed this more than I thought.*

"Juliana."

Gah. Mid-sip, I choked, and my eyes went wide. *Holy hell, I guess we're doing this, and with our full, formal names too.* "Anabella." In the chair opposite me, my twin sat wearing a smile identical to the one I'd given the life-giving barista a moment before. Even given the passage of time, sitting across from her was like looking in a mirror. She was even dressed as I was, in a light-weight cream sweater and black pants. But twins weren't meant to be carbon copies of each other, at least not on the inside.

Even so, her thick curtain of dark brown hair, almond-shaped eyes lined in a smoky-gray liner, and bee-stung red lips were uncanny. The minimal amount of makeup I wore was replicated to perfection on her face. But she didn't want to be me, not really.

Panic spiraled through me, and I dropped my gaze to the cup in my hand in horror. *Had she…?*

"Relax. I didn't poison your drink." Bella chuckled. "That would have been too simple."

Throwing caution to the wind, my gaze strayed from my attention-demanding sister and searched every inch of the café for anyone that could help me. When she followed my perusal, mocking me no doubt, I slid my phone from the tabletop and put it in my lap, hitting record.

Only the barista was in the café with us. Bella grinned. "I wouldn't, if I were you. I'll hurt her."

I couldn't have another innocent person harmed on my account. I gulped then, with a shaky voice, asked the first question that popped into my head. "How did you get past security?" I needed to keep her occupied, and there was nothing more that Bella liked than talking about herself.

"Easy. In appearance, we're identical." She pursed her lips. "And I took that broken keycard you had in your junk drawer. Didn't take much to have it replaced, and I had access to everything in your office. Your research, workstation, assistant… even your boss."

"We had the security clearance changed."

A muscle jumped at the corner of her mouth, the only indication of a challenge to her scheme. "That was unfortunate. But there were ways around that." She held up her thumb.

There was a barely discernable silicone coating over her finger.

"You used my prints?"

She answered with a smile, and I could only assume she'd gotten my print from a glass or something I'd touched and had it duplicated. *Should've gone with a retina scan.*

Do I want to know? My gaze skimmed over her identical outfit, and the pieces fell into place. "The screen saver. That was you?"

She snorted. "Of course. It was generous of me, wouldn't you say? I gave you a warning not once but twice. Actually, three times. I thought the clocks stopping at 7:16 was a nice touch."

The time of *her* birth. "The shower? You wrote on the mirror that morning?"

"I was inside your house. You never suspected. And the guards were a piece of cake to fool." She paused for a beat. "Most of them, anyway."

"What do you mean 'most of them'?" I had to stall. I didn't know what she would do.

"There was one who seemed smarter, more intuitive. I didn't go anywhere near him when I entered or exited. But other than that, getting into your house was easy. They thought I was you."

"Why? I don't understand. You have your own life in Italy. Why would you care about me over here?"

A deep-pink flush climbed Anabella's cheeks, and daggers shot from her narrowed eyes. "You had Mom, and now she's dead. You stole all those years with her when she should have been with Dad and me."

"I didn't steal Mom. She took me away because you're a psychopath. What the hell is wrong with you, Bella? You're my twin," I whisper-yelled at her.

An emotionless shield dropped over her face. If I had to guess what she was masking, it was rage. I'd pushed her, called her out on her shit. In a flash of clarity, I remember doing that once as a kid. It hadn't ended well for me. She'd shoved me off my bike into a pile of gravel—thankfully not in front of a car, but it had been bloody and painful all the same. After that little show of who was in charge, I'd fallen in line like the dutiful younger sister she liked to remind me I was.

"Get up."

Bella's words cracked like a whip across my skin. I slipped my phone in my pants pocket. Since I hadn't gone to my office yet, I didn't have my lab coat on. I hoped she didn't notice the phone's outline, but I wanted to keep recording her. If I could have, I would have sent the file to Trev.

I leaned back, defying her despite the goose bumps that

erupted over my skin in anticipation of her reprimand. "Why? Where are we going?"

Her lips curled into a menacing grin, and her eyes had the crazed gleam I'd learned to fear. "Remember that knife, the one I used to carve your arm up? I kept it."

All the blood left my face, and tingles stabbed my fingers from the memory of when she'd sliced me open.

"It's in my hand. If you don't want to die here and now, get up."

She didn't bluff. I'd learned that about her in our younger years. I stood, whispering a prayer to my mom in my mind that Bella wouldn't stab me in the back.

Behind me, she directed where she wanted me to go. We got into the elevator and headed to the twenty-third floor, the one above my lab. Silence stretched between us until I couldn't stand it anymore. "Why did you kill Fran?"

"Because she was your friend, not just your assistant. But that shouldn't be the way of things. You shouldn't exist. Fran and I had a few too many glasses of whiskey that night. I got to see how much you meant to her. It was easy. After she passed out, I marked her like you. With the same scar, I was sure the cause of her murder would point to you. That was me being humane a second time." Bella sneered. "You would've ended up in jail but still alive."

Anger skated along my spine, and I choked down a bitter cocktail of horror and grief—it wouldn't serve me well. I was older and no longer living in her shadow. Not only that—I wouldn't back down. "Bullshit. You are not God. I have a life that you're not part of. Why did you have to come here?" I let a sliver of disdain drip from my words. "We don't need to be in each other's space anymore. Our parents made sacrifices so we could grow up apart and have full, healthy lives."

"I'm surprised you believe that. You're a copy of me, a mistake. There can only be one of us, and it will be me."

"That's insane." We stopped, and the elevator doors

whooshed open. No one was in the hallway. It was weird, but it was after most people started work, and I wasn't familiar with the floor. It held offices that weren't associated with the laboratory facility—it was an IT department.

"Get off the elevator."

I stepped off. She moved to my side. It was my only possible opportunity to drag my phone from my pocket. Thank God it was still recording. With a few moves, I opened up the messenger app and shot off a quick text to Trev: *SOS. Roof.* I couldn't risk any more explanation or she might have seen what I was doing. With a flick of my fingers, I slipped my cell back into my pocket. We'd arrived at the stairwell door.

She tilted her head, indicating that I should enter. Memories sharpened, as did the horror of reliving them. I guessed where she wanted to go. We'd had a tree house as kids.

With Bella prodding my back, I shoved open the heavy steel door to the rooftop. A stiff wind whipped my hair around.

Bella had a viselike grip on my wrist, anchoring my light sweater in place. There was a strong chance it wouldn't end well for me.

THIRTY

ALL IT HAD TAKEN WAS one glance at the message Jules had texted. The two words she'd sent seared in my brain. They'd conveyed everything I needed to know. Her twin had found her, and they were on the roof.

An arctic chill pumped through my veins as I sped through the city streets to get to Jules. After one look at my face, Connor had told me to get out and do what I needed to. I would have even if he hadn't. Omar was in good hands and would soon be in cuffs at the police station.

Please let me get there in time. In front of the office building, I slammed on the brakes, put the truck in Park, and was out the door. I raced inside. Josh's eyes went wide.

"Roof access?" I didn't have time to explain. I didn't need to—he knew who I was.

"Get off on twenty-three and take the stairs." The security guard waved me through.

After I passed him, I shoved in between the elevator doors as they were closing. My heart pounded, and my skin felt stretched too tight over my body. There were two people in the cramped space with me as I hit the number for the floor I wanted. They shrunk back, putting as much space between us as the four walls permitted.

The motor whirled to life, and the elevator sped upward. We stopped for their floor, and I growled at them to get off. They slipped past me, maintaining their distance. As they were getting out, I drilled my finger against the panel. I hit the close-door button repeatedly. The doors slid shut. *Finally*. In a matter of seconds, I was out of the elevator and on the designated floor. The stairwell entrance was marked, and I took off for it, gun in hand. My shoulder and hip slammed into the metal. The door burst open, and I took the stairs two at a time. At the entrance to the roof, I slowed, inching it forward on the off chance I could take Anabella by surprise.

No. My gaze locked on the two women, hand to wrist and facing one another, inches from the roofline. It was impossible to tell who had whom because they wore identical outfits and their hair was done the same way. Because of how they held onto one another, I wasn't able to see even a hint of the scar.

I know Jules. My mind warred with my racing heart. Another second passed, then they turned to me. Tension lined the corners of both of their mouths.

Christ! Their hair was even the same length. I took a cautious step forward. "Jules, Bella."

"Trev!" The twin on the left yelled. "Help!"

"No." The woman to the right's eyes widened. "It's me. I'm Jules."

My skin crawled at the game Anabella played. Accusations filled the air between them. I ignored their protests. Instead, I focused on their posture and their facial expressions, trying to glimpse Jules's scar. I had to be sure.

I took another step forward. The door clicked shut behind me. I caught the barely indiscernible narrowing of the woman on the left's eyelid. I shifted the angle of my gun to cover her.

"Stop!" Her hands tightened on the other woman.

I froze. I was ninety percent sure the woman on the left was Anabella. She pulled the other woman closer. The other's thumb shifted, trying to force back the fabric around the woman's sleeve on the left. *Jules is on the right.*

Jules, the twin on the right—I was calling it—whispered to

Bella, and she jerked her focus back on her sister. *Thank you.* She was giving me an opportunity.

I had to be careful. I inched forward, barely noticing the distant sound of cars buzzing below. A slight breeze blew, ruffling their hair. My movements were slow, measured. Locked together, they hadn't yet moved in either direction, toward or away from the ledge. I couldn't risk charging them. Bella's state of mind was off, and if she pushed Jules over the edge, given that we were almost thirty floors up, she would die instantly upon impact.

One wrong move, and they could both die. I took another step closer. About fifteen feet separated us. Jules had pushed the end of Bella's cuff another few millimeters. The sleeve Bella held on Jules hadn't moved an inch. I got Jules's message. A bracelet, identical to the broken one Jules had on her dresser, dangled from Bella's other wrist.

"You." Bella's head whipped back to me. "Back the hell up."

"Let her go, Bella."

The lines bracketing Bella's mouth deepened. The muscles in her shoulders tensed. *Shit!* Jules pushed back, hard, and freed herself. Shock widened Bella's eyes. *Didn't expect your sister to fight back, did you?* I was so damn proud of her.

As Jules turned to me, my heart stopped. Bella recovered from the stumble. Malice transformed her face, and she shoved Jules, attempting to push her over. I pulled the trigger. As soon as the bullet left the chamber, I pushed off the balls of my feet, lunging for them. Everything seemed to happen in slow motion.

They screamed. The bullet pierced Bella's shoulder. Bella again shoved Jules, sending her hurtling toward the roof's edge. Intent on reaching Jules, I bypassed Bella but flung my arm out. The butt of my gun made contact with Bella's head. She crumpled. Without breaking stride, I stretched my right hand out. Sheer terror was etched in Jules's wide mouth and eyes. Her body flailed backward.

My fingers curled around hers. The pop of her joints was like a shot going off. Another step, and I dropped the gun. Without my hand free, I snagged the fabric of her sweater. I yanked her close. *She's safe.* "I've got you." Holding her tightly in my arms, I took several steps to safety.

Sobs wracked her slight frame. I whispered that everything would be okay. My body shook. I'd never been so terrified in my life. Those horrifying moments made it very clear that she'd become my world.

In my peripheral vision, I sensed movement. *No!* Roughly, I tore Jules from my arms and shoved her to the ground as the sound of a gun went off. My body jerked as the bullet pierced my leg, but the pain didn't register. I weaved left, making it harder for her to take aim. The second shot went wide. Jules screamed at Bella. It wasn't what I wanted. Horror had me in a choke hold. Jules was trying to draw Bella's fire to her. I lunged. My hand wrapped around Bella's wrist as the gun went off once more. I had no idea if she'd shot me again as we fell to the ground. Her head hit the surface with a thunk. Her eyes rolled back, and I tore my gun from her unresisting grasp.

Sucking in air, I rolled to my back as Jules rushed me. She fell to the ground, pressing her hand over the bloody wound on my thigh. As I sucked in air, I reached for her hand and covered it with mine. Her sweater had inched up from the ordeal, and the edge of her scar peaked out.

I pulled my cell from my pocket. Jules kept her gaze locked on me as I called Connor to inform him what happened. An ambulance was on its way. Bella hadn't moved. I wasn't sure if she was unconscious or dead. I pressed my hand over her pulse point, and a thready beat told me she lived, at least for the time being. I couldn't tell how much damage she'd sustained, but a trail of blood from the back of her head seeped onto the ground. I shifted my focus away from Bella.

"Jules." I cupped her cheek, wiping some of the tears away with my thumb. There was so much I wanted to say, but not now. Especially not so close to her crazy sister, who was lying about a foot away, unconscious but still potentially dangerous. "Let's go." I sat up and grimaced.

Tears streamed down her cheeks. "But your leg…"

"I'll be fine. We can rig the door so Bella can't get back into the building." I needed Bella to remain there until the police arrived. My only concern was Jules.

Jules slipped her sweater off, leaving her in a thin camisole. After she tied the shirt around my thigh to help staunch the bleeding, she helped me stand. The pain from the bullet wound was registering, and I fought the burn as we made slow progress to the door. With my arm around her shoulders, she wrapped hers in a viselike grip around my waist. I reached for the handle and almost fell back as the door burst open. Two police officers, their guns drawn, blocked our path. A third officer pushed through, someone I recognized from the department.

Josh, the security guard, hovered at the rear of the group, his gaze darting to Jules. I nudged her toward Josh to fill him in while I leaned against the doorframe. It didn't take long to debrief the police, thanks to Mark, the officer I was friends with. As I shuffled forward and they turned to take care of Bella, Jules reached out and threaded her fingers with mine. Even stressed, scratched up, and bruised, she was lovely.

"You're beautiful." I cupped her cheek.

She let loose a shaky laugh. "I'm a mess."

"Trust me"—I squeezed her hand—"you're perfect." *For me.*

She pressed her body against mine. "When you arrived, I was equally relieved and then terrified for you. It's finally over."

I nodded to reassure her, but it wasn't over yet.

Jules wrapped her arm around my waist. We made our way to the elevator and down to the main floor. Once there, I waved away the paramedic. I would go to the hospital and have the bullet taken out, though I would have preferred talking Jules into doing it to save me the hassle, but she'd been through enough for one day.

Before leaving the roof, an officer had checked on her sister. She was alive. We would cross the next bridge soon enough.

EPILOGUE

FIVE MONTHS LATER

THE SUN WAS HIGH IN the sky, casting rays that reflected off the water like a million sparkling diamonds. Even with that view off the balcony of my—no, *our*—San Francisco beach home, it couldn't compare to the stunning woman who stood mesmerized by the sight before her. It made sense for Jules to move in with me after her sister was charged with murder and multiple counts of aggravated assault, among other things. Carl had recovered and apologized profusely for his behavior toward Jules, which was caused by Bella messing with his head. Omar had been admitted to a mental hospital and would serve time after grief counseling.

Thankfully, there wasn't a biowarfare threat, because things could have turned out badly. My gaze strayed to Jules again. I loved that she was with me every night when we went to sleep and that we woke to start each day together. My beach house was much larger than hers, and it was a fresh start for her and for us.

With a shove, I opened the double sliding-glass doors that merged the living room with the outdoors.

Jules turned at the commotion, a wide smile curving her full lips. "What are you doing?" She waved to the room behind me. "It's cold out here."

"It's February and sixty-one degrees." I wrapped my arms

around her sweater-clad form and drew her against me. "It's warm."

She rose to her toes and pressed a kiss to my lips. "Now it is."

"We leave in fifteen minutes." It was our first vacation together. The trip to Maine didn't count. She worked too hard, but her hours did help to ease my mind when I went on missions. I knew she would be busy.

Then there was Becs, her best friend who'd moved into her house when Jules agreed to live with me. A position at Zen Pharmaceuticals, Thorn Pharmaceuticals' competitor, had opened, and Becs had snatched the job to be closer to Jules. "Is there anything else you need before we go?"

"Just you."

I tucked a piece of silky hair behind her ear as her arms squeezed my waist.

"I can't wait. Fourteen days in the Cook Islands sounds like heaven." Her fingers trailed through my newly short hair, and she laughed, the corners of her almond-shaped eyes crinkling. "I'm still getting used to this."

I grinned as her fingers tugged on the strands by my neck. "It was time. Why don't you do a quick check to make sure you have everything, and then I'll carry our bags out to the car?" With reluctance, I released her from my embrace. I couldn't get enough of her.

"I'm going to call Becs. I'll only be a minute," she called before she disappeared into our bedroom.

"Make sure she got the plane ticket." I'd sent her a ticket for a flight out of California so she could join us. Hayden would be there too. He'd had a thing for Becs ever since he'd met her after visiting us a few weeks before. I was glad he'd forced his way onto the trip—he'd be useful for keeping Becs occupied when Jules and I wanted time alone. It would mean a lot to Jules to spend some time with the woman she thought of as a real sister, and I would do anything for the woman I loved.

She poked her head around the corner of the living room as I was securing the patio doors, her cell pressed to her ear.

"Becs said she's all set but wanted to confirm you'd fly her back."

I nodded. "She's good. We're all leaving together." I was flying the Gray Ghost company jet we kept in California for me to use. Becs and Hayden would come back with us when our two weeks in the islands were up.

I followed behind her, grabbing her bags. I'd already packed, making sure to secure my gun and ammo in a carry-on bag. The time away from work was welcome—all I had to do was check in on Hannah's pet project, which Keegan was supposed to do, but he was on a mission in Venezuela.

Jules and I would have the entire vacation to do whatever we wanted, which would be a ton of water sports combined with dining out and drinking at the swim-up bars. After reading the letter from her mom and regaining her lost memories, her intense fear of the water during choppy waves and potential storms had greatly reduced. It had given her a sense of closure, which was good, as we would be in the water a lot on our vacation.

I stored our luggage in the back of the Range Rover as Jules locked the house. Her grin spread from ear to ear, and mine did too. Before I could open her door for her, she wrapped her arms around my neck, lowered her eyelids, and parted her lips. My heart rate spiked, and desire flooded my system. The woman had the power to bring me to my knees with one look.

"Have I told you lately how much I love you?" Her voice was soft, raspy.

"Not in the past half hour." I cupped the side of her face. "Hearing you say that never gets old. You're the one for me, Jules. I'll love you for the rest of our lives."

JULES

ONE WEEK LATER

A SOOTHING BREEZE RUSTLED THE palm leaves that surrounded the overwater bungalow Trev and I had for a too-short two-week stay. The first seven days had passed quickly, and I wished we could remain there for a month. It was paradise.

"Here you go." Trev placed a glass on the table in between our lounge chairs.

I curled my hand around the cool glass and took a sip. "Wow, that's good. Mango and orange juice, and is that champagne?"

He grinned. "A little. Goes with our day of relaxation. Unless you want to schedule something?"

My gaze skimmed over Trev's lean, tan body. Looking at him would never get old. I think his muscles had muscles of their own. I took another sip of my drink and checked out his hair. He had one of those faces—seriously, he could have been a model. It didn't matter if he had a man bun or this shorter-on-the-sides, slightly longer-on-top style. I loved both looks.

"Jules."

Shoot. He'd asked if I wanted to do anything. "No. I'm good. We've already done so much. It's nice to take it easy and relax." I crossed my ankles, getting more comfortable on the lounge chair. The deck was suspended over the water, kissing the edge of the Aitutaki Lagoon.

We'd packed a lot into our first week. Each day, we'd embarked on something new, along with swimming in the stunning blue water. The first day was snorkeling. Then we hiked Mount Maungapu, where we picnicked amidst a panoramic view of the island. We'd bicycled around the island in search of ancient temples and spent an entire day being ferried around on a catamaran, with stops at some of the small islands that dotted the South Pacific Ocean. We'd windsurfed and enjoyed a night at one of the resorts, where islanders performed traditional dances.

Trev linked our fingers as the water lapped below us. Content, I let my eyelids drift shut. I think I even dozed for a few minutes until the sound of his voice roused me.

"Jules." He tugged gently on my hand, his voice close to my ear. "Let's go for a walk along one of the sandbars."

"Mm, okay. Now?" He seemed on edge, energized, and so at odds with my lazy demeanor, but I could get motivated for a walk. There were many golden sandbars, and we'd talked about strolling on the one closest to our hut but hadn't yet.

"Yeah, now. I can't sit anymore." He stood, gathered our empty glasses, and took them into the small but high-end kitchen. It seemed odd that the hut had such nice appliances, but I was more than happy with them.

I rolled to my feet from the dais and trailed after him.

After rinsing out our glasses, he turned to me, his mesmerizing eyes sparkling. I needed to cool off. "Want to jump off the deck and go from there?" There was a drop off our hut's back awning, but the sandbar was only a short swim away. He drew me in for a kiss, and I melted against him. *Best vacation ever.*

Trev stepped back then grabbed my hand and tugged. "Yep. Let's go."

I picked up my pace to keep up with him, snapping out of my sleepy state of mind. Back out in the sun, he turned to me with a mischievous grin I knew too well. Hands at my waist, he tossed me in. I came up sputtering as he jumped in beside me.

I laughed. I couldn't help it. Trev was fun, and I'd been getting warm lying in the sun. I wore my new white bikini that he'd insisted on buying when we'd first landed in Rarotonga.

After I dipped back under to push the rest of my hair from my face, we swam to the nearby sandbar and waded through the water until it only covered about midcalf on me, less on him. I threaded my fingers with his, something we seemed to do more often than not, at least on vacation, when he wasn't always on guard for potential danger, needing his hands free in case something went wrong. Not only that, but I felt lighter and freer after processing where the majority of my fears regarding the water had come from.

Early evening sun glinted off the warm turquoise water, and I wished I'd thought to bring my sunglasses. I stumbled over the sand, and he chuckled beside me before slipping his arm around my waist. Slanting him a quick glare, I resumed my search for seashells. I had quite a collection going already.

Comfortable silence stretched between us despite the strange energy I sensed rolling off Trev in waves. Maybe a half hour passed, and the sun started to sink beyond the horizon. "Wow, that's so beautiful."

When I turned to him, I smiled.

He wasn't watching the sunset. His gaze was fixed on me. "I love you, Jules." We paused, and he cupped the side of my face then brushed his lips over mine.

My arms came up around him as he deepened the kiss, and we missed the last few minutes of the sun's descent. It was worth it. When he drew back, his hands fell to my hips. We stood that way for a few seconds before he slipped his arm back around my waist, and we resumed our walk. *What was that?*

I could make out a walkway of sorts with poles in a path along the sandbar not too far ahead. Lanterns hung from each one, and a group of people I couldn't make out yet stood in a half circle at the end.

"What's going on?" He'd already planned so much for us to do, and I couldn't imagine what was next. He didn't say anything, but his hand tightened on my hip. "Trev?"

As we drew closer, I could make out a few faces. Becs was standing next to Hayden, whom I expected to see the next day. I loved her pink floral bikini, and she was snuggled right up to Hayden. Good for her. "They flew in early?"

"Yes."

I glanced at him again. He was being oddly tight-lipped. Some of the people from his team were there, too, the ones who weren't out on missions—Mari and Chris, Liv and Liam, and Connor too. The week was going to be a lot different than I'd thought.

We walked along the line of glowing lanterns until we reached the end. Everyone was a little farther off. Trev nudged me so that I was facing him. *What's going on?* Then he dropped to a knee, and I froze. *Was he—?*

"Jules."

A tremor shook my hands until he took them in his. I couldn't speak, but I didn't think I was supposed to. My gaze locked onto his, and I waited anxiously for his next words.

"I've never met anyone like you before. Immune to me, for one." He winked.

I laughed. That was so true, from his perspective and to my denial, at least in the beginning. It hadn't taken me long to see past his pretty exterior.

"You're smart." He cast a sly glance at Chris. "So much more than my brother." That got a laugh from our friends. "Seriously, though. I think I knew you were the one from the first moment."

"The first?" I raised an eyebrow. I couldn't help it. We'd first met when he flew me to Washington DC.

He chuckled. "Even then, though I didn't recognize what the feelings were. But definitely when I fished you out of the water."

Tears misted my eyes, and my voice came out just above a whisper. "I think I knew then, too, though I wasn't ready to admit it to myself." *How did I get so lucky?*

"You're so beautiful, both inside and out. Everything I am, everything I have, is yours. I want to share the rest of our lives together. I want to give you the world, be there for you in every way."

He already is. This man. He is everything to me.

"Will you marry me?"

God, yes! "Yes." I wrapped my arms around his neck, and as he stood, my feet left the sandy bank. My heart swelled to bursting. Our friends converged and cheered. Hugs were shared, and then I was pulled into Becs's embrace.

"You weren't kidding," she whispered in my ear.

I knew what she was talking about. "Doesn't fit into the DC Comics or Marvel category you were going for, but then again, neither does Hayden." Becs's tendency to label guys in terms of their counterpart superheroes was hilarious.

"Oh, but he does." She flashed an evil grin. "Thor. I'd say he resembles Chris Hemsworth."

I rolled my eyes at her. It was better than encouraging her.

"I'm so happy for you, Jules."

I squeezed her again, and then Trev drew me to his side, which was exactly where I wanted to be.

He nuzzled my neck, eliciting chills. "What do you say we come back in three months and get married here?"

Twist my arm! "I'd have to say yes."

In a few short months, we would promise ourselves to one another in paradise, and I couldn't wait for our return.

Wow! Trev and Jules took me for a wild ride with challenges at every turn. Did you figure out who was behind most of the things that happened to Jules? Or maybe there were a lot of questions along the way, adding new paths and suspicion—I hope so!

I love it when the plots in movies and books unfold and the pieces fall into place like a puzzle. With that in mind, please don't share any spoilers, so others can have the same experience.

If you loved Trev and Jules's story, I hope you'll consider leaving a review on the platform where you purchased it. Telling friends and leaving reviews about an author's book is why we are able to do what we love—thank you so very much!

Curious about the vacation Jules and Trev take and who he meets with for Hannah? Find out in *Moonlit Mirage*. Or do you want to know more about Keegan and the mission he was on that prevented him from being present at the proposal or unable to check up on Hannah's protégée? The novel *Marked for Death* is Keegan's story, and it's filled with high-stakes action.

All my best,

Amy

If you enjoyed reading Covert Threat as much as I did writing it, I hope you'll consider leaving a review.

ACKNOWLEDGMENTS

Trev's book was a long time coming. I started writing Covert Threat a year before its release. The outline was completed and twenty thousand words in when I received requests from readers for Hawk's story. So I switched to Hawk.

Months later, I dove back into Trev's world but had a hard time writing. In talking with a good friend and excellent beta reader, Maryellen Newton, she brought up the issue of thawing permafrost. And there it was. I had a new plot thread that held my attention.

Even so, it wasn't smooth sailing from there. Problems arose where I tried to wrap my brain around some of the science, and I have to say I'm so lucky that Audrey Anhalt had the patience to explain the parts that were confusing in a way I could grasp.

It seriously does take a village, and I'm so grateful to all those who had a hand in bringing this story to life. I have amazing critique partners who are also super talented authors —thank you, Kristin Kisska, and Emily Albright for being there with me every step of the way and sharing invaluable thoughts and opinions that made this story better.

With every new book release, I'm fortunate to work with Taylor Anhalt, a gifted author, and editor whose editorial input makes my books shine. I value the days we hang out and write together at Panera, getting in dedicated writing time, and high word counts.

To my family for their encouragement, support, and unwavering belief. For their patience and understanding when general chaos reigns. I can't imagine life without them.

To the fabulous team at Red Adept editing—Kate B., who has worked on my books for the past couple of years, and

Laura B.—who makes the process as the book nears publication seamless and enjoyable.

T.E. Black Designs, who did the cover design and formatting, you are a dream to work with, and each project exceeds my expectations.

Last but certainly not least, a special thank you to all the bloggers and readers who have encouraged and helped me along the way, and who continue to make my dream a reality.

Thank you.

ABOUT THE AUTHOR

Amy McKinley is the romantic suspense thriller author of the Gray Ghost Novels, Moonlit romance series, the Five Fates paranormal romance series, and several standalone books. Her edge-of-your-seat books are filled with surprising twists and just the right amount of heat and danger. She lives in Illinois with her husband, two daughters, two sons, and three mischievous cats.

You can find her at www.amymckinley.com

Subscribe to Amy's newsletter for cover reveals, book announcements, and giveaways:
http://eepurl.com/dEBqJn

facebook.com/amymckinleyauthor

twitter.com/AmyMcKinley7

instagram.com/amymckinleyauthor

pinterest.com/amymckinley7

OTHER BOOKS BY
AMY MCKINLEY

Gray Ghost Novels

Moments That Define Us

Broken Circle

Eye of the Storm

Beneath the Surface

Vantage Point

Covert Threat

Marked for Death

The Five Fates Series

Hidden

Taken

Stand-Alone

Shattered Melody

Siren's Call: Cursed Seas

9 781733 942553